MW01708021

King Lester The Groovy

The Blunt City Chronicles, Volume 1

Enrico Picchi

Published by Enrico, 2025.

KING LESTER THE GROOVY

First edition. May 8, 2025.

ISBN: 979-8230797081

Written by Enrico Picchi.

Also by Enrico Picchi

Steampunk Blues
Steampunk Blues TenebroCity

The Blunt City Chronicles
King Lester The Groovy

The Paramount Sagas
Baroness

The Vigor Crystal Chronicles
The Petulant Robot

Watch for more at enricopicchi.com.

Table of Contents

To Realization,

Because acceptance is a powerful tool.

Creator and writer: Enrico Picchi

Graphic design: Aurora Giampaoli

Copy edit: Aaron Redfern

ENRICO PICCHI

KING LESTER THE GROOVY

The Blunt City Chronicles

The Blunt City Chronicles:

King Lester The Groovy:

Chapter 1: Law Clerk by Day:

Lester shuffled the stack of file folders and pulled out the horrid khaki coloured one. *The colour says it all*, he thought. He grimaced and looked at his watch. Ten to six, way past quitting time, but the snobby junior partner Michael Warner had been on him to finish organizing the latest documents for the big client meeting on Monday. Lester sighed, opened the file folder and began flipping through the documents. After a minute he wanted to storm into Warner's office and throw the heavy folder in his face. Lester didn't have time to stand when he heard the deliberately dragging steps on the moquette.

"Hey Jiggleprice," Warner said. "Have you organized my file, yet?"

Lester looked up at the broad shoulder, square jawed, blond-haired model of a lawyer. "Warner, you know my last name is Wrigglesworth." Lester glared. "Your joke wasn't funny the first time, so what makes you think it'll make me laugh after a thousand times?"

Warner sneered. "Did you organize my file, *Jiggleprice*? The big meeting is at 11 O'clock on Monday." A smug look expanded over his marblesque jaw line. "And it's not my fault you were given two last names. What kinda fucked up family do you come from?"

Lester Wrigglesworth hated both his names. His archaic first name – which for any other functioning adult would have been a last name – caused confusion. His actual surname got him laughed at from kindergarten straight through high school. He solved university teasing by dropping out his second year swearing he never would become a lawyer. Now he worked for them.

"Warner, it's six o'clock on a Friday. I'm not going to sort out your sloppiness now." Lester dropped the file on his desk and smiled at the satisfying thud. "You did your normal half-assed job of mixing everything together, just to fuck with me."

"I'm the lawyer and you're the clerk. It's your job to do the secretarial work." Warner pointed a manicured finger at Lester's head. "You got that, sheepdog? And cut your fucking hair!"

"If you want to ask the secretary to cut her hair go talk to Michelle's over by the front desk." Lester pointed across the hall. "Well, she was sitting over there half an hour ago. It's six O'clock, Warner. You can go fuck yourself."

Warner kicked the side of the cubicle with an alligator skin shoe. "Hey, manservant, I can get you fired for talking to me like that."

"No, you can't, *Biff-o*." Lester stood up and grabbed his tight, leather jacket. "Your family name might be on the wall, but you're a junior partner. You don't count for shit in the law firm."

"You better watch your mouth, *Jiggleprice*." Warner leaned in to look down on Lester. "And don't you ever call me Biff-o again. It's Michael to my friends, but you can call me Mr. Warner. Just like you used to call my dad."

"Well, Mr. Warner, your five-thousand-dollar suit is blocking my way out of my cubicle." Lester stared into Warner's eyes. "Move."

Warner looked at his gold watch. "It's two minutes to six."

"Exactly, quitting time for us *manservants* was five thirty pm. Sharp." Lester looked around the empty cubicles, hoping to find a kindred soul to witness the next events. Warner had a temper, and Lester didn't like the way he eyed the potted plant. Lester relaxed his shoulders when Warner stepped back with his eyes on the Simon Harris' door.

"I'm going to be watching you, Jiggleprice." He allowed Lester just enough space to squeeze out of the cubicle. "Eleven o'clock sharp on Monday morning. You had better have all my file in order."

"Yeah, yeah." Lester eyed the heavy pot and fought the urge to say *buh-bye, Biff-o*. "You'll get it, Warner. It's my job."

Lester walked down the corridor and swiped his badge at the glass doors. His heels clacked on the polished tiles and he strode briskly to the elevator. He swiped his badge again and pressed the down button. With the offices nearly empty, he only waited a few moments for the doors to slide open. Lester stepped inside, pressed the lobby button and smiled. Not even Biff-o the Blowhard could ruin his evening now. It was Friday night, the best night of the week.

Outside the air was brisk and the skyline was lit orangey-red and darkening. He checked his cheap, digital watch and figured he had time for a shower and shave before dinner. He dodged the honking, downtown traffic as he jay-walked to the subway stop and descended into the underworld of Blunt City, his adopted home of the last few years.

Newspapers and flyers blew around him as the gust of wind signaled the arrival of the subway car. He had to push to cram himself in with the other passengers eager to leave the sterile business district to the rich bankers who would spend the evening schmoozing over glasses of champagne. Not Lester. He had much more ambitious plans that he would share with is two best friends, Amy and Gunner.

***

The pub in the downtown core was packed with the usual twenty something crowd. Friday night could be hard to get a table, but Amy, Gunner and Lester had been coming long enough to guarantee they would get seated with minimal wait. The Friday night ritual was the highlight of Lester's week, and tonight's dinner was extra special with the challenge he would face in a couple of hours.

"Pass the nachos, Gun." Amy sipped from her straw as Gunner stuffed a heaping mouthful of The Gong Farmer's signature Chicky-Bacqui Rancheros Nacheros in his mouth.

"Here you go, Ames." Gunner mumbled and pushed the plate across the table.

"Thanks." Amy stirred her Singapore Sling. "Les, what were you saying about Warner?"

"Fuck, what a dick." Lester clicked his tongue. "He tried to get me to do some serious free overtime to organize the mess he made of the latest O'Kelly documents." Lester adjusted his thick rimmed glasses. "But I told him to go fuck himself and strutted out of the office, disco-cat style."

"No way!" Amy punched him in the arm. "Did you really?"

"Yeah, Ames," Lester sipped on his Tom Collins. "Straight up, I did."

"Right on, my brother!" Gunner sloshed his ale on the table. "Shit! Sorry!"

Lester never had a better time than when he was with Amy Garfield and Guneet "Gunner" Singh. They had met in Blunt City University in their first year at a 70s dance competition and had been inseparable ever since. Lester still kept the competition's first prize trophy in his tiny one-room basement apartment on the top his shelf with a dozen other dance trophies underneath.

"Yeah, you should have seen the look on Biff-o's face." Lester's sipped on his Tom Collins and smacked his lips. "But I still have to clean up his shit on Monday morning."

Gunner reached across the table for another loaded nacho. "Why don't you tell the law firm to fuck off?"

"You know I can't, man," Lester slouched. "I can barely cover rent as it is on my shitty pay."

"You should've become a lawyer." Gunner winked at Amy who frowned.

"Yeah, thanks dad." Of the three, Lester was the only dropout. Gunner had finished his degree in computer science and Amy was completing a post-doc in medieval history. Lester had worked at odd jobs for a while, then a few years ago he took a job in the law firm as a clerk. He couldn't say he hated the job, but when he daydreamed about his future in his cube he often was filled with thoughts of dread. Lester kept at it because he had a knack for the work and he needed a steady gig to afford to live in the downtown. Even if his apartment was hardly more than a cold cellar, Lester was close to all the major discotheques.

"Just hang in there, tiger. Something better will come along." Amy gave him a goofy grin. "And think of tonight's 70s Groove-a-Thon Contest at the EP!"

Lester's face spit into a wide smile. "Yeah. I'm taking the crown, guys. I can feel it."

"No way, man." Gunner wriggled his shoulders. "I'm been practicing all week in front of the mirror."

"Let's see if you can coordinate your stringy legs with my trademarked *Huh-Chas*." Lester snapped his fingers and thumped out a disco rhythm on the table as Amy and Gunner laughed. Tonight was the night; Lester could feel it.

Chapter 2: Disco King by Night:

The Electric Poohbah was steaming and rippling with energy. The EP was the biggest discotheque in Blunt City and held the best monthly 70s dance contests. It was converted from an old sugar factory that was located down on the waterfront and was surrounded by pubs and restaurants with a subway stop close by. The giant discotheque had several dance halls, with the central dance hall dedicated to 70s music on Friday nights. Busy every weekend, the Electric Poohbah had its most sparkly crowd for the monthly Groove-a-Thon Contest where it crowned a single winner king or queen.

Lester pushed his way through the crowd to the center dance floor for his warm up. In less than twenty minutes the contest would begin, and he was in the second batch qualifying round with Amy and Gunner. He felt the raw energy as he was bumped and jostled. Amy grabbed onto his shirt as he squeezed through a line of loiterers that ringed the dance floor. He grinned at his two companions when his heels clacked on the flashing, glass floor lighting of his warrior's arena.

Gunner hadn't been the only one practicing for the dance-off. Lester had been working hard for a month, since his second-place finish in the last month's contest. No one remembered the runner up, he thought. Lester was determined to become this month's Monarch of the Disco. He knew that for Amy and Gunner it was only a fun past-time, and even though the practiced they didn't have Lester's single-minded objective to become someone great through disco dancing.

The foggy heat had Lester sweating from his brow even before he broke out his first moves. Lester had taken lessons in high school; break dancing, hip-hop and jazz, but never felt those styles fit his persona. He knew he had been born in the wrong decade, as everything about him screamed the 1970s. His shaggy hair, his tight-fitting clothes, his slim build and his long sideburns which raised eyebrows in the office.

The pounding music was the warrior's call to pulse and confront his rivals. Lester began to circle, warming up with his disco shuffle. He quickly moved on to the low roll and then the high roll as he continued to shuffle to the center of the dance floor. He caught the eye of some long-time dance challengers. Lester shuffled out of sink and hit the counter beat opposite them before he clicked his disco shoes and flourished with a couple of high double disco-points to their howls. Tonight was the night.

Round One was up, and Lester kept his hips moving next to Amy and Gunner on the edge of the dance floor and surveyed the challengers. No serious rivals in this batch. He was certain he wouldn't have any trouble with his own round, but the real challenger was last month's winner, Ralph "The Manakin" Greenbaum. Lester spotted his shaggy nemesis across the floor standing in the Round Three group. He dressed in his usual baby blue shirt and black slacks and an orange suede cap. The reigning EP dance king was chatting with his 'chickadees' when he caught Lester staring. Greenbaum circled his arms around two of his chickadees and made a big show of laughing. Lester snapped his fingers, shook out his shoulders and took his turn on the floor with Round Two group.

Breath, hip, pulse, roll. Lester was in full groove in the middle of his qualifying round and moved on to a slick single-single-double-freeze. With a heel click he spun and galloped around the square to the cheering cloud. He stopped next to Amy for a hip bump and dared to slide away on his knees before he hopped back up on his heels. Lester grinned at Gunner as they exchanged swipe-tap-rolls. He rolled his shoulders and shimmied with mincing steps. Lester moved on to a low step knee and shook his head at a palpitating Gunner. Too early for the Huh-Cha. Lester needed it in the qualifying round to make the tete-to-tete grand finale against Greenbaum.

Greenbaum glared as Rounds Two and Three crossed paths. "Come to get you skinny ass kicked again, Les?" He sneered. "You look like a frilly cocktail toothpick."

"Your fat, feathery ass is mine, Manakin." Lester double-flicked out a roof-on-fire. "I'll see you in the finals."

Despite Greenbaum's tubbiness, Lester was impressed by his moves. He used his belly to his advantage, as every hip thrust had twice the weight behind it and he sent the girls flying. Greenbaum was surprisingly agile, and despite being short he could stretch his body and disco finger with the best of them. Lester wasn't surprised he hadn't pulled out his number one move, "The Manakin", just yet. Like Lester, he would save the big guns for the final qualifying round.

Less than an hour later the judges had picked the qualifiers. Amy was out, but both Gunner and Lester had made the Final Eight. It would be a dance-off with a jury to decide the two finalists and this month's Monarch of the Disco. The qualifiers strutted around the LED dance floor which pulsed to the pounding rhythm from the enormous speaker cabinets. Lester crossed eyes with a grinning Gunner. They turned and bustopped each other as Lester kept on eye on Greenbaum. With a nod to Gunner, it was time to seal the deal.

"Huh-cha!" Lester swept his leg in a high arc over Gunner's head.

"Huh-cha!" Gunner responded a little too low and grazed Lester's shaggy bush.

The crowd around the dance floor erupted into hoots and hollers as the final four were called out. Gunner cursed up a storm at being eliminated, so Lester was left to face off with two disco tenderfoots and The Manakin. Lester was certain the two unknowns would crack under the tremendous EP pressure, but not the Manakin. They were given just enough time to gulp down some water as the DJ changed to a more upbeat tune as the four faced off.

"Give it up, Les." Greenbaum dogged back and forth, his arms rolling to the rhythm. "Once I let loose The Manakin, he's gonna shit all over your shaggy head."

"Manakin, my Huh-Cha is gonna defeather your chicken." Les snap-kicked. "And just wait to see what I've got in store for you for the finale."

"You've got nothin', Les." The Manakin twirled. "Your Huh-Cha may have got you this far, but you'll up when you see my warp-speed Manakin."

"I'm gonna skewer your bird."

The four finalists circled and broke into coordinated dolphins, paring up, breaking off and repairing. As Lester and Greenbaum crossed over, they funky chickened. Lester readied to carwash away but was hit with a full force of a Greenbaum hip bump that sent him flying into the banister. He gestured angrily to the judges who shrugged and pointed to the DJ. Lester looked up to see DJ Funky Fuzz unfold a sheet of paper.

"Stone foxes and Casanovas, welcome to the Electric Poohbah!" DJ Funky Fuzz howled.

Lester felt a charge run through him as the discotheque exploded in a chorus of voices and booming bass notes. The crown did its typical wave and roll while marching on the spot to return the greeting. Lester had his arms above his head and sneered at Greenbaum. He tried to find Amy and Gunner on the sidelines, but he was blinded by the flashing lights.

"Tonight, we are going to crown our King! You all know these two boogie-cats!" Lester felt himself flush as he saw the DJ look right into his eyes. "I wanna see you buggin' out for Lester the Groovy and The Manakin!"

Lester and Greenbaum whooped and slid into the center of the dance floor, parading like peacocks. Lester greeted the crowd with an electric slide, while Greenbaum went with a classic hustle. The two disco warriors faced each other and unleashed a furious blur of savage points and violent hip thrusts as the club disco cats bulged and surged.

"If you ain't jivin' yet, you better get your buzz on for these two cats!" DJ Funky Fuzz slid up the dial and the bass boomed. "Give these princes your good vibes! Tonight, we crown our Disco King! Let the grand finale begin!"

The two bitter adversaries began to circle with a coordinated shimmy, each man guarding his secret weapon closest to his disco innards. Lester felt confident, he had shown his Huh-Cha, but he hadn't busted out the highly classified, extended version with its astounding finish. He needed strategy to get Greenbaum to commit to The Manakin so he could follow up with his winning card. Lester learned from his second-place finish that it was the last move that would influence the judges and bring upon complete, untamed victory.

Greenbaum and Lester faced off and began robotting. Lester shuffled left as Greenbaum shuffled to his right. They used their static, broken limb dance to pump up the crowd. Lester went with a classic 70s step, but Greenbaum dared to push the dance towards 1980. Lester recognized Greenbaum's widening stance and loose, Egyptian arms and he tensed waiting for his opponent to make his move. Suddenly, The Manakin! With a blinding side to side movement, Greenbaum broke out his signature tropical bird dance to the roaring crowd. Skipping along like a Jesus lizard across a spectral pond, the chubby reigning king dazzled the crowd. Lester waited for Greenbaum's final pirouette and tensed to strike.

"Huh-cha, Huh-cha!"

Lester arced out two sweeping high kicks in a sumptuous display of brutal masculinity. As his right foot skimmed the flashing floor like gazelle prancing across kaleidoscope, he propelled himself upwards on the tip of his toes. With a grunt he executed a perfect split jump and fell into a languid hanuman asana with his arms extended to nirvana.

"Pizzazz!"

The discotheque popped like an overflated confetti filled balloon with Gunner and Amy shrieking on the edge of the dance pit. A grinning Lester leapt back up on his feet and did a running man victory lap around the center of the dance floor as hands pounded him on the back. He hustled up to Greenbaum who tipped his suede hat in a gentlemanly gesture. Lester knew the crowd had decided the winner. He looked at DJ Funky Fuzz who spoke with the jury and pointed below. The sonic guru lifted the mic to his lips and turned to the swelling crowd.

"Funky sisters and brothers! All hail your winner and new King of the Disco, Lester the Groovy!" DJ Funky Fuzz waved to Lester as the crowd screeched and bellowed. "Lester the Groovy, come on up here and take your crown!"

Lester bounded up on the stage and waved to the thundering crowd. He did an electric slide across the stage and then strutted back while mixing in a bit of sprinkler so he could stop and admire the swarming disco cats. Lester grinned widely at the house Disco Fox dressed in a shimmering, silver desk as she approved with a plastic, gold and jewel encrusted crown. He mimed a robot sink so she could easily put it on her head and gave her his best diamond smile. Lester did his second side leap of the night and basked in the howling hubbub.

"Lester, what do you want to say to the crowd?" The DJ stuck the mic in his face.

"All hail King Lester the Groovy!" The crowd whooped back *all hail King Lester the Groovy* as Lester hustled.

"Real cool, cat! Lester, thanks for coming up! Now let's get back –"

"Flash mob on Sunday at noon in Captain Blunt Plaza!" Lester held on tight to the mic.

"Right, great. Now let's back to –"

"Your kings commands you!" Lester screamed into the mic. "Be there or be square!"

"Ok, Lester, that's enough of –"

"All hail King Lester!" Lester tore the mic from the DJ's hands. "All hail King Lester the Groovy!" The crowd roared as the DJ clawed back the mic. Lester rotated his wrist in a perfect royal wave to the chant of *all hail King Lester the Groovy.*

Chapter 3: Flash Mob:

The Burnt Toast Diner bustled with frenetic brunchers lining up to scoop mushy eggs and bacon onto plates piled high with pancakes drowned in syrup. Servers swept up and down the rows of tables pouring weak coffee and clearing off tables to prepare for the lunch crowd. The greasy spoon was located in the heart of Blunt City, right across the street from Captain Blunt Plaza, the hallowed meeting place for all career flash mobbers.

"Guys, I'm totally wrecked." Gunner's sloppily wrapped dastar slid into his eyes.

"No kidding, Gun." Amy tapped her forehead. "You drank like a fish two nights in a row."

"I know," Gunner groaned over a half-eaten plate of greasy sausage and eggs. "But we didn't really get to celebrate Les's victory on Friday night, so I had to double down last night." He raised his mug of coffee. "All hail King Lester the Groovy."

Lester raised his mug in return and grinned. "All hail me! Guys, do you think there will be a big turnout for the flash mob?" He looked at his digital watch. "It's in fifteen minutes, but I don't see anyone in 70s jive. I really want at least one hundred people."

Amy looked out the diner window. "Well, it's still early. Wait a minute!" She pointed. "Look at that group over there by the statue."

"I don't see any 70s cats."

"No, not the Captain Blunt statue," Amy pushed Lester's head to the left. "Next to the tiny, First Nations statue."

"Shit! Yeah! There must be about twenty of them!" Lester pounded Gunner on the back. "C'mon Gun, finish your breakfast!"

"Jesus, Les, take it easy!" Gunner stuffed a sausage in his mouth. "My head feels like an elephant walked all over it."

"Well, you better be ready to do the EP Line Hustle in ten minutes." Lester stood up and grabbed the powerful boombox. "Guys, can you cover breakfast? I'm going to meet and greet."

"No worries, man." Gunner yawned. "All hail King Lester the Groovy."

Lester chuckled as he danced around a serving girl and out the door. He jaywalked past irritated motorists and sashayed into the large square. Lester made a beeline directly for the group of cool cats that stood next to the muddled artistic rendering of the First Nations people. Before he reached them, he saw a lanky girl wave at him. Lester paused and wondered if he had been recognized because of his face or because of his boombox.

"Hey, you're Lester the disco King, right?" A young woman in complete 70s drag smiled.

"King Lester the Groovy, that's me!" He cocked an eyebrow and raised his slight shoulders. "You recognized me?"

"Sure, I was at the contest Friday night in Round One." She did a dolphin. "But I got eliminated in the first round."

Lester responded with a funky chicken. "What's your name, foxy lady?"

She giggled, "I'm Katie."

"Nice to meet you, Katie." Lester looked around and waved at her friends. "Not a bad group you've got."

"Thanks, but that one is way bigger." She turned to the green patch at the edge of the plaza and shouted. "Hey guys, over here! King Lester's made it with his boombox!"

Lester's jaw dropped as nearly one hundred people in full 70s threads cheered and waved. The group moved forward in a variety of shuffles and hustles as more 70s cats began to fill the square. Lester turned when he heard hollering to his back as another group with boas and suede caps shimmied towards them. He waved and arm and was met by cheers.

Lester turned to Katie. "How is it so many people know about the flash mob?"

"Your win at the disco Friday night went viral. Everyone saw the splits. It's called the Pizzazz, right?

Lester grinned, "Yeah, that's right!"

Katie clicked on her smartphone and held it up to Lester. "This is the video I posted of you on Blather. And your shout-out for the EP Hustle Flash Mob has been chirped like a million times."

"Yeah, that's me!" Lester watched his perfectly executed Pizzazz loop on Katie's smartphone. "I haven't been on Blather since Friday night before I won."

Katie laughed. "So old school. I check Blather like every five minutes. I even have automatic chirps enabled."

"I think I'm gonna check Blather way more often." He spun a 360 and kicked up his heels. "Holy shit! More people are piling in!"

Katie nodded. "The whole Electric Poohbah disco group on Blather said they would come."

"Seriously?" Lester widened his eyes. "There must have been a thousand people at the club that night!"

She winked, "yeah, so you better give us good directions, King Lester."

Gunner appeared beside Lester and shook him hard enough that he lost balance. "Holy shit man! There are hundreds of people in the plaza all decked out in 70s jive!"

"I know!" Les kept rubbernecking and saw more 70s cats arrive. "There's no way my boombox is going to be heard. Shit, I won't be seen either." He propped himself up on Gunner and tried to look over the crowd. "How am I going to lead the flash mob?"

Gunner pointed to the statue of Captain Blunt. "The base of the statue is pretty wide. You should be able to manage your moves on it. Plus, you'll be three feet higher than the crowd."

"I don't know, Gun." Amy pulled on Lester's sleeve. "Les, there's a fence around it for a reason."

Lester continued to look around the square as more people piled in. He checked his watch then looked at Amy and Gunner. "I'm going for it!"

With a cat-like bounce, Lester catapulted towards the statue and hopped over the low, wrought iron fence with his boombox on his shoulder. He leapt up on the statue's base and surveyed the crowd. The biggest surprise was that right in the middle stood The Manakin with a couple of chickadees. They exchanged cool nods as a roar went up when the crowd noticed Lester under the austere Captain Blunt. Lester watched the waving sea of dancers and onlookers lay themselves out like a perfectly orchestrated cabaret. He looked at his watch; 11:59. Lester set his boombox down, turned the volume knob to max and pressed play. It squealed out and then boomed a pulsated beat as the crowd began to hop and holler.

"C'mon disco cats you know the drill! Get ready for the Electric Poohbah Hustle!" Lester shouted. "On four! One, two, three, FOUR!"

Lester dazzled into the first part of the EP Hustle, a hybrid between the classic disco line and the bus stop. He rolled, stepped and clacked and sent his disco points upwards to pierce the sky. After whirling for a minute, he began the eight-count dolphin to signal to the crowd part two of the EP Hustle, the potentially dangerous car wash hustle hybrid. To his relief, most of the enormous crowd managed the transition with minimal impact to forearms and shin bones. The sea of disco cats twirled around as Lester yelped and began the second dolphin eight-count for the grand finale. The crowd jostled into a rambunctious sneaky-deaky hustle hybrid. They disco cats slinked up and down, then left and right as Lester clapped to keep time. As the song came to an end, Lester finished with a Pizzazz to rapture of the screeching crowd.

Lester gave his funky king's wave, hopped down with his boombox and vaulted over the low fence. He was met with high fives and hip bumps as he thanked the crowd. Lester grinned his way through the disco cats and bowed when someone shouted *all hail Lester the Groovy*. The crowd took up the chant as Lester shimmied and nearly dropped his boombox as he broke out into a Russian squat dance. Lester bounced up and minced his way across the square to the corner where the tiny Amy hopped up and down waving her red scarf.

Amy jumped into Lester's arms and squealed. "Les, that was so amazing!"

Gunner bearhugged the three of them. "My groovy cats, we are totally trippin'!"

"Did you see The Manakin!" Lester slid Amy to the ground with his boombox. "The Manakin came to pay homage to the king! That's like in the Middle Ages, right Ames?"

"Uh, well, tributes did take place but –"

"Hey! That's Katie!" Lester waved both arms furiously. "Katie, over here!"

Katie sauntered up with her bell-bottom jeans, crop top and short leather jacket. "Lester, that was totally funky! I can't believe that so many people actually kept time!"

"Yeah, I know! And there were no broken bones during the carwash boogie!" Lester slid between his best friends. "Speaking of boogie down cats, this is Amy and Gunner."

"Hi, I'm Katie." She gave a little wave from her elbow.

"Yeah, we figured that out when Casanova here drooled out your name." Gunner jerked a thumb at the glowering Lester.

Katie laughed and gave Lester a timid glance. "Well, Lester sure knows how to get his groove on."

"You should see him when he gets aww sooky sooky! Ouch!" Gunner rubbed his arm and shrugged at a frowning Amy.

"So, anyway," Lester scowled at Gunner then smiled at Katie. "So, you had a groovin' time?"

"Yeah, it was totally fab."

"Maybe we can meet up?" Lester flushed and turned his back to Gunner who tried to ogle over his shoulder. "You know maybe grab a bite, confab, and then hit the EP?"

"Yeah, that'd be great." Katie rocked from side to side. "So, you'll chirp me on Blather?"

"Yeah, right on. Like, next Friday?"

"Ok! Awesome," Katie pointed to the crowd behind her. "Well, I gotta go, but I guess I'll see you soon?"

"Right on!" Lester said, "Catch you on the flip side."

"Ok! Bye!" Katie turned giggling to her friends as the groups waved to each other.

"Wow, Lester, she's pretty cute." Amy nudged him and winked.

"Yeah man, you gonna get your groove on with that lanky lady?" Gunner pumped and thrusted his hips.

"Gunner," Amy laughed. "Knock it off!"

"Guys, this is totally awesome!" Lester grabbed them in headlocks. "My life is finally coming together!"

Chapter 4: Monday Morning:

The elevator sounded and the doors opened silently. Lester strutted down the short hallway to the law firm in a perfectly ironed and tight-fitting two-hundred-dollar suit. His heels clicked on the granite to his newfound royal rhythm. Every echo was like his boombox rattling Captain Blunt Plaza. His smile didn't even fade when the Michelle scowled at him and buzzed him through the glass doors. Lester sauntered up to Michelle who pointed to the private offices. Lester frowned and looked at his watch. It was only ten to nine, but standing by the water cooler were Simon Harris and Michael Warner. Warner glared when he caught sight of Lester walking over to them.

"Good morning Mr. Harris, Michael." Lester nodded. "You're in early."

"Lester, good morning," Harris smiled. "It's a big day today. The O'Kelly party will be here at 10:00, so we came early to prepare.

Lester blanched. "Don't you mean 11:00, sir?"

Warner stepped forward. "I told you on Friday, Wrigglesworth. The meeting was at 10:00." He gave Lester a shark tooth smile. "Sharp."

Lester felt the heat rush to his head and kept his tone level. "I guess I must have misheard."

"Yeah, Wrigglesworth, you did." He gave Lester a wicked grin. "Real sloppy."

"Lester, there won't be any problem getting the last file folder organized in time?" Harris smacked his lips. "You know just how important this contract is to our firm."

"No problem, sir." Lester gritted out. "Let me just go and sort out the final documents."

"Very good," Harris nodded. "We'll see you in the boardroom in an hour."

Harris turned to walk back to his corner office and Warner took an aggressive step forward. "You had better not fuck this up, Jiggleprice."

"Warner, you're a fucking dick!" Lester whispered harshly. "You're going to screw this up for both of us!"

"No, I'm the lawyer, you're the clerk, remember?" Warner jabbed his manicured finger into Lester's thin chest. "If you don't get the file cleaned up in time, you're going to eat shit for it."

Lester's voice cracked, "sooner or later, Warner..."

"What?" Warner barked out a laugh. "What are you going to do? Cry mommy to human resources?" Warner dug into Lester's chest with another pointed finger thrust. "Or maybe you're gonna attack me with a paper clip? If you try, I'll bust your head open with my monogramed paper weight."

Warner spun on his heels and left him trembling by the cooler. Lester tried to calm his nerves as the office began to fill up with clerks. He felt the curious stares and rushed back out the glass doors past the frowning secretary and fumbled with the lock to the bathrooms. Inside he rushed to the mirror and gasped. His face was scarlet and he was bathed in sweat. He took off his jacket and unbuttoned his shirt and put it under the hand dryer. His breathing was heavy and he kicked the waste basket and cringed at the resounding clang. Lester checked his watch and shuddered. Five after nine. He swung his shirt back over his slight shoulders and began to button up as his mind raced. He had to get the job done in half the time.

Lester blasted through the door and heard the curse of a man who took stood on the other side clutching his hand. Lester mumbled and apology and raced to the glass doors of the firm and tried to smile at the frowning Michelle. He skipped down the moquette aisle and mouthed some good mornings as he sat down and turned on his computer. He stared at the heavy O'Kelly file and put his head in his hands. He took a minute to gather his courage and then plunged in.

The boisterous voices wafted across the open space and Lester looked up and cursed silently. He looked at his watch. It was 9:50, and he was about three quarters of the way through the file. There was no way to make corrections to the last sheets, so Lester furiously began to write out post-it notes to reference when the lawyers would need to look at other documents. There were too many mistakes to correct, but he figured he could just whisper them to Harris and Warner during the meeting.

His phone trilled and he looked up at the secretary across the cubicles as he picked it up. "I guess it's time, Michelle?"

"Yes Lester," Michelle's thin voice was tense. "You better get over to the board room."

"Right." Lester put down the phone and sighed as he slid the last documents into the file folder. He stood up, sucked in a heaping lungful of air and blew out sharply. He adjusted his cheap grey suit jacked and calmly walked towards the boardroom. He could see through the semi-frosted glass that all parties were seated and cursed under his breath. He knocked on the glass door and opened it until it butted into Warner's foot.

"Thank you, Lester!" Warner broadcasted to the entire law firm. "I'll just take that from you." Warner yanked the heavy folder form Lester's hands and turned to the O'Kelly party. "Law clerks, always making us sweat it out until the last minute!"

There were a few chuckles as Lester leaned his head and whispered. "Warner, I always sit in on the big board meetings to provide support regarding –"

"Thanks again, Lester. You can get back to work." Warner pushed the door shut on Lester who stood blinking, his arms hanging limply. Through the striped frosting Lester watched as Warner gesticulate like a circus clown, shaking hands and thumping backs. Lester thought back to Evan Warner, founding father of Warner, Harper & Harris. The great, stern man had always been highly professional, nothing like his buffoonish son. He caught the black look of Michael Warner as he sat down in the center of the boardroom table. As Lester turned, he noticed the conspicuous absence of senior partner Evelyn Harper from the room.

Lester plodded back down the moquette to his cubicle of shame. His eyes fell on the potted plant, and he wondered if he would have the strength to lift it to the skies and crash it down like boulder into Warner's skull. From the odd stare from his cubic neighbor, Lester realized he had been standing with his eyes on the pot for just a minute too long. He teetered into his diurnal cube and plopped down on the thinly padded chair. Slowly Lester lengthened a hand to work on the next contract, thankfully one handled by Harper.

For the next two and a half hours, a distracted Lester tried to work through the Arlington contract. Though he couldn't say he enjoyed clerking, once he got into the groove, he found he could organize, research and correct files easily. But this morning his eyes flicked up constantly to the boardroom, waiting for the moment the door opened to pounce. But he wasn't sure if he wanted to confront Warner or take his case to Harris.

Just before 12:30 when the office was about to close for lunch Lester saw movement through the frosty glass of the boardroom. He stood up and skimmed into the aisle next to his leafy, terracotta weapon of choice. The men and women began to file out with Harris in the lead, obviously taking them to lunch. Lester would have to settle for second prize as he saw Warner was clearly dallying to give him time to reach him before they left. Lester sucked in a lungful of air and marched to Warner.

"Why do you hate me, Warner?" Lester cursed himself for his inane remark.

"What the hell are you talking about, Jiggleprice? You can't hate a nothing." Warner's lip curled into a lopsided sneer. "You know, we could have ten girls in to interview for your job tomorrow." Warner snapped his fingers. "Just like that. You think about it before you go to sleep."

"I don't have to put up with your shit, Warner."

"Yeah, you do. Unless you want to do my law firm a favor and get the fuck out of here." He pointed to the glass doors. "Remember, I'm the king, not you." Warner's sneer widened as Lester blanched. "That's right, I saw your disco bullshit on Blather. Just another reason why you don't belong here." Warner looked like he was about to spit. "You're a disgrace to Warner, Harper & Harris."

Warner strode away and left Lester standing with the arms limp for the second time that morning as the office filed out for lunch. He caught a few quizzical looks from his colleagues and mumbled that he wouldn't be joining anyone else for lunch in the big food court a block from the Covenant Tower. Lester dragged his feet down the moquette and plopped down again in his poorly padded chair. He pulled his sandwich out of his small knapsack and tossed in the garbage bin.

***

Sitting in his moldy apartment, Lester brooded over a flat beer. Other days had been bad at the firm, but this had taken the cake. He hated that the conceited Warner could get to him that way, but he had never felt so insignificant. What really ate him was there was nothing he could think of to get even with Warner without losing his job. Lester looked about for his smartphone and spotted it on the bookshelf on top of a hockey magazine. As he picked it up to dial, his eyes fell on a book and he smiled.

"Hi Les, what's up?" Amy's voice was tinny through his cheap smartphone.

"Huh? Yeah, Hi Ames. It's me."

Amy giggled. "I know, Les. What's up? You sound distracted."

"Yeah, well. I kinda had a shitty day."

"Do you want to tell me about it?"

"Nah," Lester lied.

"Ok. Then do you want me to ask you questions about it?"

"Yeah." This time Lester told the truth.

"Was it Warner again?"

Lester hiccupped. "Shit, Ames ..." The levy broke and Lester flooded the airwaves. He paced around the room, at times with melancholic steps, at times stalking in anger. He kicked at the air and imagined Warner's square jawline shattering in front of him. During the incandescent rant Amy supplied the necessary gasps and mutterings to keep his tragic epic flowing. Finally, Lester drew a ragged breath and blew out hard.

"Les, I am so sorry," Amy's voice was infused with as much sympathy as Lester's lousy phone would allow. "But do you see what I mean?"

"Yeah, I think I do." Lester sighed as he scratched his head.

"Warner is totally jealous!" Amy hammered home the point almost every time Lester told a Warner tale. "He's not going to stop because he's insecure."

"But his dad is dead and when Harris and Harper are retired, he'll get everything."

"Lester, that doesn't matter!" Amys voice came and went. Lester was pretty sure she was shaking her smartphone. "He's a big, jealous baby. Warner probably sees you as the usurper."

"User what?"

"Usurper! Like claimants to a crown."

"Oh, your medieval stuff."

"Yeah, but figuratively it applies here, too." Amy clicked her tongue. "He probably felt threatened by the work you did with his dad, and now he's going to punish you."

"It's not like I'm gonna inherit Warner, Harper & Harris."

"No, but you're a constant reminder of the good relationship you had with Evan." Amy said. "You worked on the big stuff with his dad and Michael didn't. You were organized all of Evan's files until he was too sick to come into the firm."

"Yeah, I had a great working relationship with Evan." Lester leaned on his bookcase and nearly pushed it over. "Shit!"

"What's wrong?"

"Nothing! But yeah, I helped Evan close out a really big deal before he got sick all of a sudden." Lester scratched his chin. "I put in a lot of hours with him towards the end."

"You see what I mean?" Amy trilled. "Baby Warner is still jealous over it!"

"I dunno. Maybe."

Amy clicked some weird sounding buttons, then her voice returned. "Can't you go to HR about his behavior?"

"And say what? Biff-o is the dead founder's son." Lester bit his lip. "And Harris covers Warner's lazy ass all the time."

"What about Harper?"

"She's smart enough to stay out of it." Lester's voice was thick. "I see how she acts. Harper says her good morning to Biff-o and then she disappears into her office. She wasn't even in the O'Kelly meeting this morning."

"Mm-mm, mm-mm, I see." Amy's voice was suddenly perky. "Hey Les, do you want hang out tonight?"

"Nah," Lester lied again.

"Are you sure? I can call Gunner and we can meet at The Gong Farmer for dinner."

"I don't want to be a ball and chain ..."

"No! You're not!" Amy put a silvery cheer into her far away voice. "I'll call him right now."

"I dunno ..."

"We can meet for dinner and take your mind off it." Amy bubbled. "I'll call Gun and fill him in so you don't have to say it all over again."

"Ok." Lester smiled. "Thanks Ames."

"Sure." Amy used her goofy voice. "We'll cheer you up, tiger. Promise!"

"Great. So, The Gong Farmer in an hour?"

"Yeah. If I don't chirp back anything different on Blather see you there in an hour."

"Bye Ames."

"Bye Les."

Lester tossed his phone on his used love seat and out of the corner of his eye the book caught his attention again. His finger lightly touched the spin and he slid out the picture book, a gift from his mother when he was a boy. He grinned when he looked at the title; *Frederick, the Little King That Could!*. The cartoonish boy on the cover with an oversized crown smiled back at him as Lester looked at his disco crown sitting on the top shelf.

***

Chapter 5: Planting the Seed:

Monday evening at The Gong Farmer was dead quiet. Two bored servers walked up and down the empty tables and grumbled about tips. The big screen TV replayed the sports highlights and the small one scrolled out natural disasters, wars and a nose-diving stock market. When the platters hit the table Amy and Gunner stopped their argument long enough to smack their lips.

"I know all there is to know about my religion." Gunner rubbed his hands over his BLT.

"What are you talking about, Gunner?" Amy made her trademarked 'what-are-you-talking-about' face. "Isn't Sikhism a dharma? It's not a Western style religion."

"Yeah, that's what I meant." Gunner bit into his BLT and mmm-mmed. A look of serene peace spread over his face.

Amy pointed at Gunner's plate. "Gun, you're eating bacon."

"So what? There's no agreement about eating processed meat." Gunner mumbled through a mouthful. "Uh, right?"

"Gunner, I had to help you learn the Kirtan and your family's Raga because you were always at hockey practice!" Amy flurried her hands. "If it hadn't been for me, you would have missed last year's Vaisakhi."

"It was April." Gunner mimed a wrist shot. "We needed to prepare for the finals."

"Geez, Gun, your mom was so mad!" Amy tapped her head with her index finger in her trademarked 'you-just-don't-get-it' gesture. "Remember? I had to take the subway all the way uptown to the rink and drag you out of the changeroom!" She covered her face. "With all those half-naked guys. It was so embarrassing!"

"C'mon Ames, we made the finals last year!" Gunner grimaced. "But we lost to the fucking Giffins. I had to eat shit twice. Second place and my mom pissed off about Vaisakhi." He mimed his mom's wagging finger. "She went on about it for the whole summer."

"Gee, I wonder why she was so upset?" Amy smushed up her face and crossed her eyes at Gunner.

Gunner was about as un-Sikh as a Sikh could get. He ate Kutha, wore a sloppy dastar, shaved his beard off in the summer, got drunk on the weekend and had virtually no knowledge about his dharma's rites. As a teen he was nicknamed Gunner because of his wicked slapshot and not even his dad called him Guneet anymore. To the fury of his mother, he ditched every festival he could for hockey. Ice hockey, ball hockey, street hockey, roller hockey. If it meant swatting at a puck or a ball, he was on it. If it hadn't been for a nasty ACL tear in his second year in university, Gunner had a chance to turn pro.

"This year's gonna be different." Gunner munched on some chips.

"Well, I hope so." Amy bit into her tuna melt.

"You gotta see our new goalie." Gunner slid back and forth in a T-push on the booth seat. "He can stop a low wrist shot like nobody's business."

"You're hopeless, Gunner." Amy threw up her hands. "Hopeless!"

"Guys, I've been thinking." Lester said as he cleaned off a fried wing. "You know. About life and stuff."

"Uh-oh," Gunner elbowed Lester. "The king's about to go philosophical on us."

"I'm serious, Gun." Lester rubbed his eyes under his glasses. "I mean, I'm not doing anything with my life."

"That's not true," Amy said. "I know you had a really bad day today with Warner, but something better will come along."

"Yeah Les, Amy told me about it. What a dick." Gunner grabbed his knife and thrust it forward with two hands on the ends. "If his shitty team makes the playoffs and our divisions meet, I'm going to cross-check his ass even if means getting red carded."

"You'd do that that for me, man?"

"Totally, man."

"No, Gunner! Guys, no!" Amy stood to give them a shake with her spaghetti arms. "That is exactly how *not* to solve a problem."

"Yeah, you're right." Lester sighed. "Then Gunner won't have a chance of winning next year's local cup."

"That's not what I meant, Les." Amy sighed. "Anyway, you don't have to keep working there forever."

"Yeah, don't sweat it, man." Gunner took a swig of his ale. "You'll blow them off sooner or later. Plus, you've got the weekends."

Amy smiled, "and you've got us."

"Yeah, I know." Lester pushed aside his plate. "But I'm really stuck in a rut. I feel so sluggish during the week. I'm only living for the weekends."

"That's kinda normal, Les." Gunner put a hand on his shoulder.

Lester stared at Gunner. "Gun, you don't have a daddy's boy dickhead shitting on your parade every day. Plus, you like programming."

Gunner shrugged. "Well, alright, I have a pretty good office environment. But my job is only job. It's not like I'm playing center in the NHL."

Lester turned to Amy. "Ames, you love your job."

Amy gave him her goofy look. "Yeah, I do. I've always been a history buff and I can research in the university and get paid for it." Amy smiled from ear to ear. "I can't wait for September. A full semester research grant to study the Cathars in Occitanie!"

Amy Garfield had graduated with honours and had never left the university. She finished her doctorate in medieval history and continued researching on grants. Amy had already traveled twice to France for research and her talent scored her an assistant professor's job as soon as she had her PhD. With flexible hours, Amy was able to pursue her other passions, sewing and disco dance.

"You see what I mean?" Lester tapped his fork on the table. "What do I have? Biff-o?"

"Well, what do you want to do?" Amy squeezed his arm.

"I want to be King."

Gunner chuckled. "You already are, man. You're the King of the Disco!"

"No, I mean I really want to be king." Lester gave them a level look. "I want to be the King of Blunt City."

Lester watched them impassively as they both laughed until they stopped dead, eyebrows up to their hairlines.

"What the hell are you talking about, man?" Gunner shook his wrists Italian style.

"You guys saw the flash mob, right?" Lester said.

"Yeah, Les, we were there." Amy sighed. "I think I know where you're going with this, but you should stop before you fill your head with crazy ideas."

"I mean, Captain Blunt Plaza was jammed." Lester's eyes were alight. "I told the people to show up, and they did! Way more than I ever expected."

"Jesus, Les, it was only a disco flash mob." Gunner shook his head. "You're not some fucking messiah."

"You're right, I'm not." Les tightened his jaw. "I'm the King."

"Actually, they're the same thing but that's a whole other history lesson. C'mon Les," Amy put her head on his shoulder. "I'll help you put your CV together so you can get out of the law firm."

"I don't want out of the firm." Les crossed his arms. "I want to rule it."

Amy tugged on his hands to break his defiant stance. "Les, they aren't going to put you on the board of directors."

"Maybe I just have to figure out how to become the King of Blunt City." Lester looked calmly at his two musketeers. "Then who is going to stop me?"

"Lester!" Amy gave him a shake. "I know you too well. When you get those crazy ideas in your head you take things too far. You need to stop now."

"Yeah, Les." Gunner gave him a nudge. "You know I'm just teasing you about you about being a lawyer. Just forget about Biff-o and let Amy help you find another job."

"So, Ames," Lester said. "How do I become king."

"Lester, no! Stop it right now!" Amy blew out a sigh.

"Isn't' that your job?"

"No, Lester! I'm a medieval historian specialized in French and English wars and political conflicts!" She tapped her forehead. "I'm not a kingmaker."

"Well, someone made them."

"Yeah, Les." Amy sighed. "Noble families and bloody wars made the kings."

Lester sipped his Tom Collins. "So, how do I become king?"

"Lester! Lester!" Amy's reedy arms flailed. "You can't become king for so many reasons it would take me the whole night to explain it to you."

Lester shrugged. "I've got time."

Amy blew out an even noisier sigh and gesticulated to Gunner who pulled on Lester's sleeve. "My man, listen to me. We know you're upset. Today was a really bad day, we got that." Gunner pointed back and forth to Amy. "But before you plan one of your crazy things, you should probably listen to Amy."

"I am listening." He turned to Amy. "So, Ames, how to I become king?"

"Aarg! Fine! Let's do it this way. We'll meet again next week and I'll bring a stack of books to show you why it will never happen." Amy snapped her twiggy fingers. "Lester, are you listening to me or are you lost in your little world again?"

"I'm listening, I'm listening."

"Good. Next week I'll bring a stack," Amy mimed a cube with her elfish hands. "A big stack of books to show you that you will *never* become king of Blunt City."

"Uh-huh."

"Lester!"

Chapter 6: The Return of the King:

Friday night the Gong Farmer was a push-pull of patrons. The shouts from the university crowd over cheap pitchers of beers blended in with the savvy conversations of the twentysomethings talking about careers moves. The bartenders poured pint after pint as the servers whirled by with platters of pub grub for the hungry patrons. Sitting smack in the middle of the chaos, Lester and Katie sipped on their drinks.

"This is a really cool place," Katie turned around and gawked at the bar. "Wow, they have a ton of beers!"

"Yeah, that's why Amy, Gunner and me come here to The Gong Farmer." Lester said. "It's got Gunner's favourite ales."

"You guys come often?"

"At least every Friday night." Lester pointed across the room. "Our usual table is over there."

Katie turned. "Yeah! That's a cool, cozy corner booth." She squinted. "Isn't that Amy and Gunner over there right now?"

"Yeah, that's them." Lester waved and Amy responded with a furious flutter of her tiny hands. Gunner grinned and raised his pint.

Katie shifted uncomfortably. "Uh, do you want to go sit with them?"

"Nah. I wanted to have some time to chat with you, my boogie down cat." Lester mimed a sprinkler. "We'll groove with them later at the EP."

"Oh, ok," Katie laughed and cast a dubious eye across the room. "Alright then."

"So, I saw on Blather that you work downtown, too." Lester gulped his ale.

"Yeah, I'm in the business district. Oh, food's here!" Katie shifted back as her order of fish & chips and Lester's burger and fries arrived.

"Yeah, we're only a few of blocks away from each other." Lester bit into his burger. "We should meet for lunch somctimc."

"Sounds great!" Katie bit into a fry. "So, I'm a marketing assistant at the Appropriation Brothers Bank."

"That's the big stone building with the gargoyles on it."

Katie giggled. "Yeah, that's the one. What do you do?"

"Law clerk. I work for the fat cats over in the Covenant Tower."

"They're probably not as fat as mine!"

Lester grinned, "Yeah, probably not that fat." He looked up to see Amy and Gunner standing over them.

"Hi Katie!" Amy waved.

"Hi Amy! Hi Gunner!"

"Hi Katie," Gunner nodded. "Listen guys, we're going to head over to the Electric Poohbah and try to get in before they charge cover." Gunner winked. "I'll get us a romantic table for four."

"Cool, man." Lester raised his pint. "We'll see you in a bit."

Katie watched them walk away and turned to Lester. "Are they together?"

"Nah. We're the three amigos." He frowned. "But not in any weird way."

Katie laughed. "It's ok, I know what you meant. They seem really cool."

"Yeah, they are. Gunner's a cool dude and Amy's great at solving problems." Lester looked over his drink. "She's going to help me with a big one."

"Oh yeah? What problem is Amy going to help you solve?"

"She's going to help me figure out how to become the king of Blunt City."

***

The line in front of the Electric Poohbah snaked around the pylons and infront of the chic restaurant next door. The crowd was a mix of 70s cats and hip-hoppers, most in their mid twenties. The line moved quickly as the multiple cashiers took money, stamped hands and ushered the kids indoors. Katie and Lester reached the front of the line, and the doorman nodded at Lester and waved them in past the register. Lester and Katie shrugged unanimously and smiled at each other. The checked their coats and Lester's money was waved away when he tried to pay. He grinned at Katie, picked up their jacked tokens and walked into the sizzling discotheque.

"Wow, you got the VIP treatment!" Katie gave him a nudge.

"I know, it's crazy!" Lester shouted. "It pays to be king!"

She laughed shyly, "looks like I picked the right guy."

"And I chose the right queen!"

The two laughed and arm and arm then entered the main hall to thunderous disco music. They shoved their sinuous bodies through the mass of people and Lester steered them to the left where the tables were located. He squinted in the dim light until he saw a tiny flurry of hands at a small, round table with a couple of love seats. He took Katie's hand and slithered around the head bobbing lounge sitters until he reached Amy and Gunner sipping on drinks.

Lester squeezed on the seat with Katie "Hey guys, do they serve here or do we have to go up to the bar?"

Gunner pointed to the bar. "I'd go get one. It'll take the server an hour to get back to our table."

Lester turned to Katie. "What are you drinking?"

"I like a daiquiri, but aren't we gonna dance first?"

"Hell ya! Let's go!" Lester jumped up and did a quick robot to the giggles of the group. Lester led the charge onto the main dance floor and skipped across the flashing lights. He turned and grinned as they formed a circle and dogged back and forth to the pulsing beat. Lester dolphined around the three and stopped to hip bump Amy and Katie. He caught the eye of the Manakin with his chickadees, and they exchanged regal nods.

"Katie and I are going to go to the little girls room." Amy screeched.

"Sure, Les and I will bust a move for you." Gunner wobbled out a Charleston as the girls laughed, then disappeared into the crowd. Gunner and Lester continued to bob about and found themselves invited into the Manakin circle, where Lester tipped his imaginary hat to the man's orange suede one. They lead the group in a slick hustle as a crowd formed around them.

Lester was in full boogie mode when a tiny hand grabbed him roughly and yanked with a jarring, one-hundred-pound force. "Lester!" Amy shouted in his hear. "What is the matter with you?"

"What," Lester frowned. "Just because I'm the King doesn't mean I can't funky chicken with The Manakin."

"No, Lester! I talking about your pipe dream about being king!" Amy held on to his shirt collar and yelled. "Why did you tell Katie that I'm going to help you become king of Blunt City?"

"Well, aren't you?"

"No, Lester I'm not!" She shook his arm. "I said I was going to show you that it's impossible!"

"Where is Katie anyway?"

"She's over there talking with some of her disco friends." Amy's short arm pointed behind her. "Why did you tell her you want to be king?"

"Because I do."

Gunner shuffled off the dance floor and shot the two a perplexed look. "What's wrong, Ames?"

"It's Lester!" Amy punched him in the arm. "He told Katie that I'm going to help him become the king of Blunt City!"

Gunner blinked twice to digest the news. "Dude, are you fucking insane?" Gunner shook his whole body. "I mean, Amy and I know that you're crazy, but do you have broadcast your bizzarro ideas to Katie on your first date?"

"I'm not crazy." Lester said.

Gunner put his hands on his hips. "I think the jury's out on that one."

"We just need a kingly plan."

"No, Les." Gunner double shook his index fingers. "We do not need a kingly plan. We need to get you out of the law firm and into some other place where you can think straight."

"Yeah, Les." Amy pushed her head into Lester's shoulder. "I mean, Katie is really cute and really nice, but you're going to scare her off. I had to tell her you're a practical joker."

"But I'm not."

"I know, Les! Aargh! Gunner!"

"Dude, my man." Gunner swung a muscular arm around Lester's skinny shoulders. "You're totally stressed and we dig it. And we want to help you. But if you keep shooting your mouth off like this your entire world is going to blow apart."

Lester was silent as he looked at his two confidents clinging onto the slick rock of hope. "Ok."

"Oh, thank god!"

"But on Monday I want to look at those king books."

Amy bared her teeth. "Fine! But don't invite Katie or you'll screw everything up." She sighed. "Lester, when you see it's impossible for you to become the king of Blunt City, will you stop?" She snip-snapped. "Lester, are you listening to me?"

"I'm listening, I'm listening."

"Aargh!"

"Shit, man." Gunner shook his head. "You're really gonna make us sweat this one out."

***

The night wound down and the four walked to the exit of the Electric Poohbah as the lights came on and the music slowed. Amy and Gunner slid off to the side so Katie and Lester could exchange an awkward goodnight. They mimed Blather chirps with their thumbs as Katie walked away with a group of her disco friends. Amy tugged a grinning Lester towards the nearest subway station.

Gunner split off from the Amy and Lester in the tunnels to take the interchange which went uptown. Amy and Lester took the nearly empty subway to the city center in a sleepily silence. Amy hugged Lester at the Blunt University stop and skipped off to her private dorm room on the scholarly grounds. Lester continued one more stop to the outskirts of the downtown to reach his disco den.

Up the subway steps, down the street and towards his apartment. The air was cold and damp and Lester grimaced at the thought of his own clammy apartment. He rounded the corner of a side street and walked down the stairs to his fox den. He fumbled out his keys and twisted his way into the tiny cellar and pushed the door closed with his shoulder.

Lester clicked the lock shut and threw his keys on the coffee table. He turned to his skinny bookshelf and ran a hand over the boy king and stopped at a giant tome. The massive birthday gift from Amy a few years back dwarfed the Blunt City phone book. He heaved it off the shelf with a grunt and thumped it on the coffee table. *A Brief Encounter with World History*. Lester opened the book flipped to the end. The page number 1548 was a challenge he wasn't ever sure he could accept. He stood up and pulled a slim book off the shelf and smiled at the title; *Exciting European History!*. It had been a gift from his mom when he started high school. It had 247 pages, but he remembered there were a lot of maps and pictures.

Lester flipped to the chapter on medieval history and skimmed through to the section on kings. He frowned. There was no mention of how to become king. He looked through the table of contents and found a section on noble lineage. He started to read until his eyes began to cross a minute later. Lester sent a private group message on Blather to Amy to remind her to bring her kingly books on Monday. He was messaged back tiny, red frowns from Amy and little, shaking heads from Gunner.

Chapter 7: The Plan:

The pile of books filled up the booth table at The Gong Farmer and threatened to spill onto the floor. Amy spread out a table cloth sized chart and pointed to the branches that crisscrossed to various boxes, triangles, circles and hexagons. She arranged the books in an order that completely bewildered Lester. while pointing to the titles. Frequently Amy stopped to frown and wave her butterfly hands to keep Lester and Gunner's attention as she lectured them.

Lester squinted at a tiny name in one of the boxes in the English Monarch's Chart. "So, maybe I descend from the Pomegranates?"

"*Plantagenets.*" Amy frowned. "Even if you did, that bloodline finished its rule over England with Richard III before the Renaissance even started."

"But I still could be noble." Lester said. "Maybe in one of the other families?"

Amy blew out an exasperated sigh. "In some way anyone of European background could probably trace some family members back to Charlemagne, and the various branches from there." Amy flipped through her notes. "But I can tell you from experience there isn't any documented evidence for most people to prove any claim of nobility."

Les grabbed a book entitled *European Nobility, Then and Now*. "But maybe the Wrigglesworth family is in here somewhere."

Amy pulled the book out of his hands. "Even if there is a Wrigglesworth family in here, I'd have to research your family's specific history to see if it is linked to a noble house." She cocked an eyebrow. "When's the last time you saw your dad?"

"I dunno. Boxing day, I think." Lester yanked the book back and flipped it open to 'W'. "You need him to figure it out?"

"Well, I need to start somewhere." Amy pulled the book back out of his hands. "Maybe your dad has some old documents that I can use to trace you ancestors back to England."

"Jesus, Ames," Gunner put down his bacon cheeseburger. "You aren't actually going help him with this, are you?"

"I'm not going to help him to become king, I'm going to show him that it's impossible." Amy picked up the monarch's chart. "I did the same kind of research for your dad, remember? He was thrilled when I traced your family tree back to 1886 in Punjab."

"Yeah," Gunner grinned. "My dad was totally stoked about it."

Lester tapped his index finger on the French portion of the chart. "But maybe somewhere back here I could actually have the right to the throne of England." He brought his nose down to the paper and squinted. "That would make it much easier to take Blunt City without the use of force."

"Force?" Gunner balked. "Les, what in the hell are you talking about? You don't really think you can put together a disco army and storm Parliament Hill."

"Why not?" Lester gave Gunner his best determined stare. "If that's what the people want."

Gunner groaned as Amy grabbed Lester's hand. "Les, listen to me; you have no claim to any kingship anywhere, let alone in Canada to take Blunt City. Or in any country in the Commonwealth. The English throne – Les, listen to me!" She lifted his chin until he looked her in the eyes. "Right now, on the English throne, sits the Windsor family. On the male side they descend from the princely Germanic House of Saxe-Coburg and Gotha." She let go of his chin and flipped open a marked page. "But it also branches out further to the House of Glucksberg through Prince Phillip. I'm not even sure if I got it all right. I'd have to spend time researching the English Royal family tree."

Lester's eyes darted over the chart. "You mean there are others who want my throne?"

Amy fumed. "It's not your throne, Les!" She pointed a puny finger at the book of modern nobles. "The throne of the United Kingdom is already complicated enough without you or other real noble houses getting involved." She thumbed through the book and pointed. "Like Jacobite claim or the House of Oldenburg, for example.

"What do the Old Birds have to do with my throne?"

"House of *Oldenburg*!" Amy twisted a lock of hair. "They would be the parent house of the branch of the agnatic line of King Charles III, but like I said, I'm not sure, I'm a medieval historian, not a modern one. The current king ascended through his mother Queen Elizabeth II because the House of Windsor is not agnatic."

Lester scratched his chin. "I thought the kings of England were Christians, not agnostics."

"*Agnatic*, Lester!" Amy tapped her forehead. "Not agnostic, agnatic! Meaning that the succession passes through the male bloodline. But that is not the case with the English throne." She pulled out another book from the pile and frowned at it. "Who knows if the House of Oldenburg could make a challenge? Some people do sustain the Jacobite cause." She massaged her temples. "Anyway, I think the English Royal family will stick with the House of Windsor. The rules of succession are super-complicated."

"So maybe I can simplify things." Les thumbed through the Amy's scholar's book. "You know, start fresh with the House of Wrigglesworth."

Amy rubbed her eyes and grimaced. "It doesn't work that way, Les. You can't just declare that your family is a noble house."

"Well, how did all the other noble families manage it?" Lester crossed his arms.

"Yeah, Ames." Gunner leaned in. "How did the others do it?"

Amy stared from Gunner to Lester. "Are you two serious? You've never cared about anything other than disco dancing and hockey and now you want me to explain European history from the fall of the Western Roman Empire up to the noble families of today?"

"Will it take long?"

"Lester! Lester! Argh!" Amy's tiny hands shook him frantically. "You have to stop before you get carried away."

"Then what happens, Ames?" Lester prepared to trap Amy through her love of history. "Let's say I can take the throne. You know, as an academic exercise. Who comes after me?"

"Well, you'd have to establish a bloodline." Amy bit her lip. "Get married, and have at least one male son that you declare your heir. Agnatic primogeniture has been a more common way of passing thrones throughout history. Your son has to outlive you so he can take the throne."

"And in the meantime?" Lester thought of Katie, his disco queen, and their future boogie-cat princeling.

"You'd need advisors and governors to help you rule over the country." Amy said. "Trusted people who can help you manage the individual provinces and territories."

"So, like us two, Ames?" Gunner rested his chin on his knuckle. "What would we do?"

"Well, historically speaking, as a woman, I wouldn't really be given much space. I'm not specialized from the Renaissance onwards to really know what kind of role I could have today." Amy bit her lip and looked at Gunner. "I suppose Lester could grant you nobility and elevate you to duke. Then you would rule over Ontario on his behalf."

"Awesome! So, I'd be Duke Gunner of the House of Singh." Gunner mimed a slapshot. "Goal!"

"Maybe." Amy shook her head at Gunner. "Edward III of House Plantagenet started it all when he named his son the Duke of Cornwall in 1337. But that was within his own bloodline. I'd have to do some research."

"What about you, Ames?" Lester said. "What can you do for your king?"

Amy narrowed her eyes. "You are in desperate need of an advisor. Historically accurate or not, I'd be your Chancellor."

"Then we have a plan."

"No, Les! We do not have a plan!" Amy shook a scholarly tome in front of Lester's face. "Noble lineage is a hugely complicated subject and you stepping in as a usurper king in a federal republic will not be accepted by the modern electorate! I can't even imagine what the Canadian authorities would do." She twisted her hair until it knotted around her thumb and forefinger. "Les, no one is going to coronate you king of Blunt City!"

"Well then," Lester pushed his thick rimmed glasses up to his forehead. "I guess I have some work to do with my people at the Electric Poohbah. Another fearless flash mob should do the trick."

Amy spread her hand over the piles of documents. "Les, you have to be more than bold to be crowned the king of Blunt City."

"King Lester the Groovy of the House of Wrigglesworth." Lester put the plastic Electric Poohbah crown on his head. "I think it has a nice ring to it."

"Lester! Lester!" Amy tapped her forehead again. "You can't crown yourself!"

"I can do it for him." Gunner reached for Lester's bejeweled, pliant garland of conquest.

"No, Gun, you can't do it either." Amy pointed at her one of the books on the pile. "The kings of England are crowned by the archbishop of Canterbury."

Lester yawned. "Well, maybe we can figure out how to fly his archbishopyness over the pond."

"Lester, stop!" Amy was back to shaking him. "There is no way the archbishop of Canterbury is flying overseas for your coronation."

"That's because I haven't taken Parliament Hill." Lester cleared his throat. "Yet."

"Gun!" Amy leaned across the table. "Say something!"

"Listen man, Amy is right. The history lesson has been fun, kind of, and I know it's been a complicated couple of weeks for you, but we need to get back to real life." Gunner mimed a backhand. "Why don't you lace up yours skates and play with us again? You were pretty good at dekes on the wing."

"I think I'll take up polo." Lester adjusted his crown. "Or jousting."

"Stop it, Lester! Stop it, stop it, stop it!" Amy flailed her arms. "Do you even know how to ride a horse?"

"It can't be that hard." Lester shrugged. "Actors do it all the time in the movies."

"Argh!"

Chapter 8: Throwing Down the Gauntlet:

The sticky note bunched up in Lester's hand. He threw it away and scratched out another note before sticking it on a document. He placed it neatly in the file folder and began skimming the next document with a red pen in hand. The desk phone trilled and Lester looked up at the secretary across the open space who pointed at her handset.

"This is Lester Wrigglesworth." Lester leaned back and twisted his finger around the desk phone's cord. "Whom may I ask is calling?"

"Don't be smart, Lester."

"Oh, sorry Michelle, I didn't recognize your voice." Lester watched the flat line of her mouth from over the cubicle labyrinth. "I thought the firm prided itself on all the smart people that worked here."

There was a moment of silence as Lester watched the irritation spread across her face. He heard an angry sigh. "Mr. Harris would like to speak with you privately in his office."

"When?"

Lester watched her frown at him from across the room. "Now, of course."

"Now's inconvenient."

"Lester, please go to Mr. Harris' office." She gritted her teeth. "Now. And knock before entering."

Lester watched Michelle slam down the phone and mumble under her breath as she angrily straightened out random items on her desk. She turned back toward him and mouthed the word *go* as she pointed frantically to the senior partner's corner office. Michelle forced a smile on her face as she buzzed in a couple of suited clients.

With as much nonchalance as he could muster, Lester slowly stood up from his creaking desk chair and stretched his arms lazily overhead. He smiled at the angry stare from the secretary as he carefully took the one and half steps to leave his cubicle to reach the corridor moquette. Lester stopped to admire his potted plant, smiled again at the fuming secretary and minced towards the Harris' hallowed door. He stopped and looked at the plaque serenely; *Simon Harris, CEO & Senior Partner*. He breathed on the bronze plate and gently buffed it with his sleeve. Lester knocked on the door as Michelle stood up with her hands in her hair.

"Come in!"

Lester opened and closed the door in one smooth motion. "You wanted to see me, Mr. Harris?"

"Yes, Lester." He waved to the armchairs in front of him. "Take a seat."

Lester sat down on the plush leather and ran a hand over the arm and whispered. "Smooth as a law clerk's skin."

"What was that?"

"I said, you wanted to see me, Mr. Harris?"

"Yes, well, how should I put this." Harris folded his hands and rested his elbows on his oak desk. "I've received some complaints regarding your work."

"Who from, sir?"

"Does that really matter?" Harris frowned. "Don't you want to know what the complaints are?"

"Not if they are coming from Michael Warner."

Harris leaned back and gave Lester a cold stare. "I know that you and Michael don't see eye to eye."

"That's one way of putting it."

"But our firm prides itself on teamwork." Harris reclined but Lester saw the tension in his shoulders. "To be successful every part of the team must to his or her job."

"Am I not doing my job, sir?" Lester drummed his fingers on the desk. "Are there complaints from any of the other senior lawyers or partners?"

Harris pursed his lips. "No, Lester, there aren't any others. But that doesn't mean that I won't take any single complaint seriously."

"Warner has been on my back since before he made junior partner and it's getting worse." Lester crossed his arms. "I'm not the only one he's picking on, but I'm his favourite target."

"Perhaps Michael is under strain given his new responsibilities." Harris leaned in confidently. "As a team, shouldn't we reach out and support him?"

"Nah, I don't think so."

Harris looked like he had been slapped in the face. "Lester, did you hear what I said about teamwork and a successful law firm?"

"I think Michael's getting it easy because of his dad." Lester pointed at a portrait that hung on the wall. "He'll never be half the lawyer that Evan was."

Lester watched Harris's face turn stoney white. "We all know that Evan was a great man and a great lawyer and he will be sorely missed."

"Uh-huh. Well, if you don't mind me saying, Mr. Harris, the late Mr. Warner treated people right. I've clerked for both Warners so I can tell the difference." Lester cast around in his mind for something he had read in one of the history books and smiled. "I think you and I both know that the apple has fallen far from the tree."

Harris' pale skin flushed from the neck upwards. "As I said, Michael has been under tremendous strain. The loss of his father last year, the role as junior partner this year." He clutched his fountain pen hard. "I think we should all bring respect to the Warner family."

"Why, are they nobles?"

"Pardon me?

"Do they descend from the Plantagenets? Is Warner an English name?" Lester pushed out his smuggest smile. "You know, the Plantagenets were originally French. They were the Angevin Empire, you see."

"Lester, I called you in here because a partner is very unhappy with your output." Harris' face trembled. "I did not call you into my office to make a mockery of our founding father."

"No, Mr. Harris." Lester held his gaze. "You called me in here to make a mockery out of me."

Lester felt the frosty wall of silence crystallize between them. Harris was immobile, his breathing sucked up in short gasps. Lester could feel the grandfather clock ticking almost as much as he could hear it. His own heart raced at the thought of his impulsive words. Lester wasn't sure if his slapshot top corner goal was an offsider.

"I believe, Lester, you should go back to your desk."

"Of course, Mr. Harris." Lester stood and felt the sweat run down his back. "I was just working on the Arlington contract for Evelyn Harper. She's expecting the reports correctly filed by the end of the day." Lester turned to Harris before he opened the door. "Let's see what Evelyn has to say about my work."

***

"You're fucking crazy, man!" Gunner shook his head and laughed. "Crazy!"

"Yeah, Les." Amy put a hand on his arm. "Don't get me wrong, I think you were right to stand up to those bullies, but don't you think you're pushing it a little?"

"I really can't take the bullshit anymore, guys." Lester clinked his fork against his Tom Collins. "I work hard. I'm never late. I clean up a lot of their shit. Even the good lawyers can be pretty damned sloppy." Lester drummed his fingers on the table. "It's time for a revolution."

"Lester, you're getting all mixed up again!" Amy sneezed. "Sorry."

"Bless you."

"Thanks," Amy blew her nose. "Les, you want to be king but you talk about revolutions. You're confusing reactionary and social change forces. These forces have always fought against each other throughout history."

"Well, maybe I can make a smoothie out of them."

"Lester, you can't blend historical change into your favourite drink!" Amy tapped her forehead. "And let's not get into this again. You will not become the king of Blunt City."

"I really think I'm only one step away. Isn't that how it happened in France? The people got pissed and bam!" He snapped his fingers. "Down with the Bastille and up with the Revolution."

"No, Lester, that is not how it happened!" Amy shook her hands to the heavens. "The French Revolution was steered by nobles and it went on for ten bloody years!" She grabbed Lester's sleeve. "Are you just cherry picking the stuff you like out of everything I gave you to read?"

"Well, yeah."

"Lester!" Amy tugged on her hair. "I didn't give you hockey magazines to flip through!"

"I know Ames, but you gave me a mountain of stuff to look at."

"I gave you books to read, not to look at!" Amy pulled harder on a lock of hair. "I gave you those scholarly texts so you can educate yourself and not repeat other people's mistakes."

"Exactly. That's why I want to mix it all together. I can call it The King's Revolutionary Smoothie." He pushed his glasses up. "I think it has a catchy 21st Century ring to it."

Amy waved her hands in front of Lester's eyes, checking for signs of human cognition. "Are you mad?"

"It'll totally work on Blather." Lesters said. "I'm sure I'll get a million chirps."

"Argh! Gunner!"

"Listen, man." Gunner grabbed his shoulder. "You're one step away from disaster. We love you, but we aren't going to be able to save your dumb ass if you do something really stupid."

"I won't do anything stupid." Lester said. "I just need to do something bold."

"What's that supposed to mean?" Gunner frowned. "I know you want to beat up Biff-o, but he's twice your size."

"That's not what I mean." Lester said. "Not yet, at least."

"Lester! Lester!" Amy headbutted his shoulder. "You can't fix the world with violence."

"I promise guys, I won't do anything crazy."

Amy and Gunner traded grimaces. Amy stacked her books on the booth seat beside her when the servers arrived with plates of food and refills for the turbulent trio. Lester ate his buttermilk fried chicken serenely while Amy and Gunner muttered into their respective Bufalo wings and steak and ale pie. The moody silence lasted half the meal, then Gunner sloshed his ale on the table and broke the lull with a mouthful of curses. Lester snorted lemony gin out of his nose and Amy laughed until tears rolled down her cheeks.

Chapter 9: Blather Will Summon Them:

The heavy history book sat in Lester's lap as he read about Charlemagne. He was truly impressed. The man had started off as king of the Franks and then became emperor. And a holy one at that. If only Lester could prove that the Wrigglesworth family was related to Charlemagne. Then he could latch onto the great man's chainmail and ride his horse to kingship. And then emperorship. And then holy emperorship. His daydream was interrupted by his warbling smartphone blasting out a tinny, 70s beat. Lester ruffled through his hockey magazines and pulled it out of the heap. He sighed as he gingerly brought his ninety-nine-dollar phone to his ear.

"Hi Ames."

"Lester, are you out of your mind?" Amy's squealy voice made him cringe.

"I guess you're talking about my latest Blather chirp?"

"Of course I'm referring to your insane Blather chirp! Les, please! Call it off." Amy strained her voice. "Call it off. Right. Now."

"I can't, Ames. The people have spoken."

"Lester, Lester, Lester! You're going to get fired!" Her voice took on a shrill pleading tone that wobbled over the airwaves. "You can't hold your Disco King's Revolutionary Smoothie Flash Mob at your place of work." She growled. "A place full of lawyers!"

Lester had pondered the decision of a flash mob at the firm, somewhat. He admitted it was more of a gut instinct than a carefully crafted plan, but his disco sense told him it was time to act. "Didn't you say I have to be bold?"

"When did I say that? And about what?" Amy's sigh sounded like a wheeze through the smartphone's crappy speaker. "Les, you could get into serious trouble for breaking into your work place."

"I'm not breaking in. It's being held Friday at noon while I'm working." He paused. "With everyone else in the office."

"Les, the disco flash mobbers don't work with you!" Her shrill voice went up half and octave. "You'll be lucky not be arrested!"

"Aren't you gonna come?" Lester touched the portrait of Charlemagne lovingly. "Katie and Gunner chirped me and both said they'd be there."

"If I came it would only be to stop you!"

"Can you put a thumbs up on my chirp?" Lester flicked a nail. "If you re-chirp it, it'll help with my Blather ratings."

"Lester, I know how Blather works!" There was a weird scratchy sound, like fabric across the mouth piece.

"What was that?"

"I'm trying on the new sweater I made!" Amy snapped. "Les, you're going to get arrested!"

"So, are you coming or not?"

"Lester..."

"Is that a 'yes'?"

"Lester," Amy whined.

Lester lowered his voice. "I scheduled it for Friday because I know you're not teaching at the university."

"Fine! I'm coming, but if I see the cops I'm out of there!"

"I dig it, groovy sister."

"Argh!"

Lester listened to the silence for a few moments then put down the phone and turned his attention back to Charlemagne. The Frank had been crowned a whopping three times, no small feat for one man. Charlemagne first coronation was as king of the Franks in 768, then king of Lombards – whoever they were – in 774. But best of all he had been crowned Holy Roman Emperor in 800, an easy date for Lester to remember.

Lester flipped forward to another favourite chapter, the artillery general and later emperor, Napoleon. He smiled each time he read 'minor noble' regarding his upbringing. It gave Lester hope. The man had probably been smaller than Lester, yet he had conquered much of Europe. Lester frowned as he remembered that Napoleon lost some nameless battle somewhere and been exiled. Then he lost again in Waterloo and had been totally screwed out of his career. But before this Lester read that Napoleon had managed to change a bunch of laws to improve life for the common folk. Lester figured he could make good use of Warner, Harper and Harris to change the laws for all of Canada. After he gave Biff-o the boot he would make him gas up his limousine.

The book slid off of Lester's lap with a thump onto the coffee table. He picked up a hockey magazine and thumbed through, but it no longer had the same appeal. There were lots of noble team colours, banners and flags, but it lacked the justice he was seeking. He had seen too many offside goals and unjustified five-minute penalties to believe the NHL was the paradise he once thought it was. He wondered if he could reform it once he became king. Surely it could do with a remake, maybe even on horseback. If only he could figure out how to put skates on horses.

Lester yawned and thought of the big day coming up. It was a gamble but now that he had his mind set on justice, he couldn't think of anything else. He admitted he had pulled a fast one on the disco cats, but when they danced up a storm, he was certain they would understand the need behind The King's Revolutionary Smoothie.

Lester threw his hockey magazine on the pile and reached to the armchair to grab his blanket. As he prepared to curl up on his futon he thought again about Charlemagne and his coronation in 800. The book said he had been crowned in the basilica in Rome. It was rather inconvenient, but maybe he could fly the pope over once he had access to a government jet. If he hurried, his own coronation would be another easy date for historians to remember. King Lester the Groovy of Blunt City, coming in late 2025.

Chapter 10: The King's Revolutionary Smoothie:

Warner, Harper & Harris was unusually busy for a Friday morning. Clients came and went frequently through the glass doors past the glacial but smiling Michelle. The lawyers and clerks hurried about, exchanging folders and chatting in the open corridors. The meeting rooms opened and closed with bustling staff and eager clients slipping in and out. Lester smiled and reclined on his stiff chair by elongating his spine. The stage was set for his King's Revolutionary Smoothie.

Lester cleared off his desk, setting his stationery in his desk and carefully placing his computer monitor on the floor. He eyed the slim table legs and hoped it would support his weight. He took his boombox out of his oversized duffle bag and heaved it on the table while casting furtive looks over the cubic maze. He would have to hope no one would come prying in the time it took him to let in the crowd that was clustered below.

The sweat beaded on his brow as he stood and took out his smartphone. Lester sent a Blather message to the EP group participating in the flash mob and he slipped into the aisle, walked briskly past Michelle, exited the doors and raced to the elevators. He jumped in and cursed their slowness but thanked the fact that Warner, Harper & Harris was only on the 10th floor. It would make sending the crowd up the fire exit a quick and viable plan.

The doors dinged and opened on the ground floor and Lester sprinted to the front desk, then slowed nonchalantly as he walked to the main doors where more than one hundred disco cats had gathered. He opened the door to a smiling Katie, a scowling Amy, and perplexed Gunner. Before Amy could open her mouth Lester turned on his heels and skipped back to the front desk and smiled at the security guard.

"Hi George," Lester leaned casually on the desk. "The Young People's Lawyer Convention has arrived. I'll just bring them up."

"A youth convention?" George frowned as he stared at his computer screen. "I don't see that on my list."

"Oh really? Well, isn't that strange." Lester opened his eyes wide and pushed up his glasses. "You mean Michelle didn't send you an email?"

"No, she didn't." He reached for the desk phone. "I'll just call her."

"Oh, that scatterbrained Michelle." Lester guffawed and slapped his hand down on the counter. Then he rubbed his fingers back and forth. "Just her typical, cranky and forgetful self!"

George smiled as he began to dial. "Yeah, she can be really grumpy."

"Remember the time when she forgot to tell you about the visit from Japan?" Lester slid a sheet of paper on the counter. "And then she got mad at you for letting them up without notice?"

"Yeah," George's finger hesitated on the buttons. "She was a real witch that day!"

"I know! It totally wasn't your fault!"

"No," George's face clouded. "No, it wasn't! I mean, I had a bunch of Japanese suits standing around. It would have been rude to keep them waiting. What else was I supposed to do?"

"I totally agree! Well, don't worry about her." Lester handed the security guard a colourful, amateurish brochure printed on Warner, Harper & Harris letterhead. "Here's the info on the event. I'll just send them up the stairs so they don't block the elevator." He winked. "Keep them young cats trim so they don't become like those fat-cat lawyers."

George laughed. "You got that straight, Les." He shook his head. "Harris has put on quite the paunch."

"Hasn't he, though?" Lester waved to the group and pointed at the stairs. "Up you go! 10th Floor, guys!"

"Oh, and Les?" George's face was a mask of seriousness as he held the phone to his ear.

"Uh, yeah?" Lester squeaked.

"I saw you on Blather!" George grinned as he put the handset down on the cradle. "I can't believe you can do the splits!"

Lester collapsed onto the counter and then raised his head with a dazzling smile. "Did you see the whole performance? I mean, did you catch my Huh-Chas before the Pizzazz?"

"Yeah, man! Your high kicks are awesome!" George snapped his fingers and bobbed his head in time. "I wish I could've been there, but the wife had been nauseous most of the day." He smiled. "Know what I mean?"

"Did she eat some bad sushi?"

"No man, she's pregnant."

Lester blinked. "Oh, right! Great news man!"

"Thanks," George's grin pushed up his chubby cheeks. "It's gonna be our first."

"Wow, that's amazing!" Lester cast an eye at the disco army column filing through the fire exit door. "So, I guess I won't see you guys for like, twenty years or so?"

George laughed. "No, it's not like that, Les. Linda just needs to settle down. We'll make it back to the Electric Poohbah for sure."

"Awesome! You know, next month I have to defend my crown." Lester jogged out a running man. "Hope to see you there, man!"

"You can count on it!" George gave him a Blather-style thumb's up.

A grinning Lester turned and bumped into a tiny foreboding cloud of turmoil. "Hi Ames."

"Lester!" Amy punched him in the chest. "You just sent more than one hundred people up the stairs with Katie in the lead! Katie, Les! The young woman that wants to be your girlfriend!" Amy punched him in the chest again. "She's all goggle-eyed over you!"

"Right! We better get moving," Lester scampered to the elevator with Amy and Gunner on his heels. He pressed the button and smiled his kingly smile at his faithful chancellor and unswerving duke.

"Lester, you're crazy!" Amy tugged on his arm. "Call it off!"

The elevator dinged and Lester dragged a clinging Amy inside as a silent Gunner trailed with a crooked smile on his lips. Lester spoke solemnly. "The people have spoken."

"Then the people are as stupid as you are!" Amy raged. "You're gonna get everyone arrested!"

"Nah." Lester said. "Trust me, Ames. I've got it covered."

"Lester," Amy headbutted his chest. "This is going to be really bad. I can feel it."

"Nah."

"Lester..."

"I'm really glad you came, Ames." Lester put his hands on her shoulders and looked into her round brown eyes.

"Oh, Lester..." Amy sniffled. "Gunner ..."

Gunner sighed and put his arms around them. "Guys, whatever happens, we're in this together." Lester and Amy snapped their heads to look at him. "Seriously, guys. Lester's plan is bat-shit insane but at this point I wann ride out the storm with the both of you."

Lester hugged the smiling Gunner and pulled a reluctant Amy into his arms as the doors opened. He dragged her to the stairwell and put an ear to the door. He smiled when he heard boisterous voices and clacking heels from the great disco beyond. Lester waved to Gunner to take his place at the door and walked towards the firm. Amy frowned but followed Lester as he walked to the glass doors and swiped them inside to be greeted by the puzzled look of Michelle.

"Hi Michelle."

"Hi Lester," Michelle stared at the 70s Amy and frowned. "Who is your client?"

"She's not a client, she's a future subject of King Lester the Groovy." Lester pulled himself up and reached out with his index finger. "Just like you're gonna be."

"What?"

"You'll understand in a minute." Lester looked over his shoulder as Michelle's eyes bugged out when the glass doors clicked opened to allow for the disco apocalypse. Lester took his finger off the desk buzzer and smiled. "It's the King's Revolutionary Smoothie, baby!"

With a bounce Lester raced past a babbling Michelle and turned the corner to dart down the aisle to his cubicle of destiny. He slid inside and kicked over his monitor to a wince. Lester stepped up on his chair and surveyed the 70s disco cats as they streamed into his office. His colleagues' jaws dropped as the crowd began to holler and dance. Lester grinned and hopped onto his creaking desk.

He raised his messianic arms and shouted, "Welcome to King Lester the Groovy's Revolutionary Smoothie!"

He was met by the resounding Blather chorus, *all hail King Lester the Groovy*! Lester bent and pressed play and his boombox rumbled to life. It blasted out a wicked 70s beat and the crowd broke into the Electric Poohbah Hustle with Lester commanding his warriors from the desk top. Lester directed his army through the motions as his desk creaked and buckled under his dancing feet. He grinned at the shocked gazes of Harris, Harper and Warner from across the room. His glorious 70s paladins bobbed and hustled to a mix of frowns, smiles, horrified gazes and laughter. Lester called the finale, leapt from his desk and landed in the corridor inches from his potted plant.

"Pizzazz!"

The 70s crowd whooped as Lester did a back spin, hampered by the clingy moquette, and hopped up on his feet to wave. He saw Katie shouting with her hands cupped to her lips, Gunner pumped his fist in a blinding vortex, and even The Manakin tipped his orange suede hat to Lester. Lester caught the eye of Amy, arms crossed and frowning. Slowly but surely, she shook her head and her frown turned upside down.

"Loyal subjects, welcome to the reign of King Lester the Groovy!" The crowd roared as he motioned for silence. "You will all bear witness to the trial of Warner, Harper & Harris!" Lester pointed towards the three scowling faces that stood in front of the boardroom as the crowd booed. "They are charged with incompetence, indifference and cover-up." The disco cats continued to hiss and boo as some of the clerks joined in. Lester motioned for silence. "I would also add psychological cruelty, abuse of power and conspiracy." He turned and gave the three a level stare. "How do you plead?"

"Lester Wrigglesworth!" Harris shook with rage. "I don't know what has come over you but I want you to know that I've called the police!"

"Mr. Harris, do you deny the charges?" Lester's voice carried over the cubes. "Do you deny that you have entrusted me to organize, adjust, redact and complete the abysmal work of Mr. Michael Warner while remaining silent about it?"

"Lester I'm –"

"Do you deny that you called me into your office to berate me on my work because said Mr. Michael Warner made a complaint?"

The roomful of clerks and lawyers buzzed. They exchanged looks and many caught the eye of Lester and nodded. His cubicle neighbour clapped him on the arm and gave him a Blather thumb's up.

"Lester, this is not –"

"Ms. Evelyn Harper!" Lester boomed. "Do you deny the charges against you? Do you deny that you have turned a blind eye to the bullying of Michael Warner towards me?"

"And me! And me!" Shouts went up from a handful of law clerks.

"Lester, please." Evelyn raised her hands as her eyes darted from frowning face to frowning face. "It's been a difficult time since Evan passed away. I'm sure if we can calmly discuss this together in the board –"

"And do you, Michael Warner, deny that you have conspired to have my work ridiculed?" Lester thundered with his arms to the heavens. "Do you deny that when I challenged you on your egregious behavior that you threatened to fire me?"

Warner ground his teeth and jabbed out a scrupulously manicured finger. "Fuck you, Jiggleprice."

The office erupted with junior lawyers shouting and a handful of clerks charged Warner who cowered against the frosted glass. File folders were launched and someone hurled a coffee mug cracked the frosted glass inches from his head. Warner shielded himself behind a shaking Harris when a voice boomed over the din.

"Alright, ladies and gentlemen! Everybody calm down!" A burly, middle age police officer held his hands up as he pushed through the mixed bunch of agitators. "I'm officer Webber, my colleague is officer Lopez. What is the problem here?"

"It's him!" Warner pointed at Lester. "He's gone crazy! He invaded the building and threatened to kill me with his band of psychos!"

Webber cocked an eyebrow at the muscular Warner crammed into his designer suit and then turned to the willowy Lester wearing his favourite two-hundred-dollar one. He grunted. "Your name, young man?"

"Lester Wrigglesworth."

"Are you bullshitting me?"

"No, officer."

"Alright Wrigglesworth," Webber put his two meaty hams on his hips. "Is what he says true?"

"No," Lester said. "I'm only overseeing the trial. I haven't picked an executioner yet."

"You see!" Warner shouted. "He's a crazy killer! Arrest him! Arrest him now!"

Webber sighed and took a step towards Lester. "You should watch your mouth. If you play it cool maybe we can just break this up and everyone goes their separate ways."

"Absolutely not!" Warner stormed over to stand behind Webber. "This is a law firm! I want him arrested and charged!"

"On what charges, Biff-o?" Lester folded his arms. "Let's hear you run them off."

"Well, uh, for starters –"

"Officer Webber," Harper strode briskly forward on her low heels and smiled. "My name is Evelyn Harper, I'm one of the senior partners. This has been a difficult morning for all of us, but we can handle the matter internally. I thank you for coming but we'll take care of our dirty laundry in house."

"No!" Warner stood beside Harper; his face bathed in sweat. "I want him arrested!" He turned to Harris. "Simon, I want Wrigglesworth arrested."

Harris flushed as he looked from Warner to Harper. "I'm sorry Evelyn, but we can't simply pass over this event. Lester has brought an unruly mob into the workplace." He nodded to Webber as the law office booed and shouted Lester's name. "Officer, please take him away."

"Alright, then." Webber motioned to Lester to come forward. "Wrigglesworth, come with us."

The room swelled fiercely as clerks pointed angrily at Warner and disco cats chanted *King Lester the Groovy*. The officers held up their hands and shouted for silence. As the din subsided a mousy voice pierced the air.

"This is totally unfair!" Amy pointed her pinky-sized index finger at Warner as the lanky Katie clung to her. "Lester is a hard worker who has been abandoned by his seniors! This whole office knows that the big, crybaby named Michael Warner is a bully!"

The office flared up with jeers as paper balls and a stapler were launched at Warner. Warner cursed and shouted at the officers to arrest Lester. Webber and Lopez raised their hands and shouted back at the crowd as the commotion died down.

"Calm down, calm down! Ladies and gentlemen, let's keep our cool so things don't get out of hand." Webber rubbed his hand over his face and muttered. "I think this is the stupidest arrest I'll ever have to make." He sighed and looked at Lester, "I know this is tough for you Wrigglesworth, but you have to come with me. Any stupid move now will really put you in hot water."

"I can't." Lester said and pushed up his thick rims. "I'm in the middle of the Revolutionary Smoothie Trial. The people haven't spoken yet." Lester smoothed out his shaggy hair, his mouth was a thin line. "I won't leave without a verdict."

Webber scowled and stepped forward. "Wrigglesworth, I'm not in the mood for your bullshit."

Lester crossed his arms. "And I'm not in the mood for yours."

Webber reached to grab Lester who stepped back and tripped over his potted plant. He tumbled and was caught by Gunner before he hit the floor. Gunner set him back on his feet and glared at the muscular cop. "Officer, Lester was just talking. There's no need to get aggressive."

Webber jabbed a finger at Gunner and took another step forward. "You stand down sir or you're going to be next in line."

Gunner pushed Lester behind him and held up his hands. "Let's just be calm about this. The man has a legitimate grievance and just wants to be heard. Let him finish the trial." The crowd shouted for Lester as paper balls lofted through the air and bounced off of Webber and Lopez.

Webber turned around and sneered at the suits and bell-bottoms. "Yeah, a real challenge." He motioned to his colleague. "Lopez, let's put these two clowns under our jack boots and get the hell out of here"

Lester and Gunner stepped back as the crowd parted the disco seas for a challenge of Davidic proportions. Lester and Gunner exchanged looks as they fell into their most menacing disco stance. Lester's hips swayed to an invisible beat, then he whispered to Gunner. "Gun, two of our classic Huh-Chas," He winked. "But just a little too low."

"Alright, you two are under –"

"Huh-Cha! Huh-Cha!"

The double whirling kicks toppled the coppers to a universal gasp that echoed through the law firm. Gunner stared at the officers rolling on the ground and then grabbed Lester's arm. "Oh shit, Les!" He put a hand to his sloppy dastar while still clinging to Lesters skinny arm. "Now what?"

"Run away!"

Lester leapt over Webber who reached out and grabbed his leg. Lester went sprawling, somersaulted and was back on his feet in an instant. With two panther-like bounds he leapt on a chair and over a cubicle and crashed through his brittle desk under a shower of knife-like file folders and piercing paper clips. He flailed his way out of the rubble, stood up and ran right into a brawny, blue wall.

"Hi officer whatever-your-name-is!"

Chapter 11: Political Prisoners:

The neon lights overhead flickered, casting morose shadows intermittently on the stained, white walls. The bars of the large common cell were painted prison grey and faced a short corridor which lead to armoured double doors with safety glass portholes. Inside the common cell two criminals waited to face justice. One paced like a caged tiger, the other sprawled like a Zen panda.

Gunner held the ice-pack to his cheek. "Fuck, man! I can't believe I let you convince me into kicking a cop in the head." He winced as he gingerly pushed the compress down. "What in the hell were you thinking?"

Lester put his ice-pack on the right side of his dark rimmed glasses where a lens should have been. "It's not like our Huh-Chas hurt them."

"Yeah, because they managed to partially block our kicks!" Gunner leaned on the wall next to Lester. "That stupid dance move could've knocked them old cold!"

"My Huh-Cha is not stupid."

"It is when used on a cop's head!"

"What else were we supposed to do?" Lester tried to keep the oppressive cell walls from swimming around him and wondered if he would have a black eye. "Amy said we needed to be bold if we were to start the King's Revolutionary Smoothie."

"Fuck, Les! That's not what she said!" Gunner stood over him. "Listen to yourself! You are not going to be king of Blunt City!"

"Why not?" Lester screwed up his face and winced at the effort. "We had a pretty good turnout for the Flash Mob trial before things turned to shit."

"Yeah, and now we're really in deep shit, man."

"The trial was nearly concluded." Lester set his jaw. "I had them for high treason."

"High treason?" Gunner's arms flailed and his compress tumbled into the crook of his elbow. "You can't accuse anyone of treason! You're not the king of Blunt City!"

"I'm almost there." Lester breathed out trying to stop the room from oozing around him. "And I thought you wanted to be duke."

"C'mon Les, it was just a game. You're fucking insane if you think you're gonna be crowned king of Blunt City. We'll be lucky to make bail." Gunner fumbled his ice pack again. "Fuck, my mom is gonna kill me! I was the pride of the family."

Lester turned his head so fast he felt himself swoon. "What the hell are you talking about? Your sister *the doctor* is the pride of the family. Your dad says you're just a bourgeois gamer."

Gunner sat down on the plastic stool next to Lester. "My dad said that?"

"Said what? Bourgeois, or gamer?"

"Both!" Gunner stood up. "Did he really call me a gamer?"

"Yeah. I heard him say it to your uncle on your last birthday."

"Oh, no way, man!" Gunner tugged on his dastar. "Shit, I write trading software for banks! It's an upstanding job."

"Yeah, real upstanding," Lester heaped on as much sarcasm as his throbbing head would allow. "Writing hedge fund software."

"Well, you work for fat-cat lawyers!" Gunner snapped. "And they just got us arrested!"

"You know what? I think I'm gonna make your dad my duke. Then your successful sister can inherit the role." Lester rolled over and felt a queasy wave. "Your dad wouldn't be shitting his pants right now."

Gunner loomed over Lester and rolled him on his back. "My dad wouldn't have kicked a cop in the head to finish up in prison!" He cocked an eyebrow. "And aren't men so supposed to inherit the role from their fathers? My sister wouldn't be next in line, would she?"

"You aren't the first born."

"Yeah, I know that. But, isn't that how Amy said it works?" Gunner scratched his beard. "You know, father to son?"

"You mean the primal agnostic thing?"

"Yeah, that thing."

"Does that mean you still wanna be my duke?"

"Fuck no!" Gunner stomped to the far side of the holding cell. "You're crazy, man."

The two fell into a proletarian silence. Gunner leaned against the wall, the compress firmly on his cheek. Lester lightly put a hand on his eye and poked through the missing lens, flinching at the pain. Lester wondered if his subjects would storm the police station. It would be his Bastille Day.

"Hey Gun," Lester tried to crane his head towards Gunner but immediately renounced the herculean effort. "I've been wondering something."

"What?"

"Do you think Napoleon was a good force or an evil force in history?"

Gunner moaned. "Fuck, Les! Would you get your head out of your ass for a minute?"

"No man, I'm serious." Lester tried to pull himself up and renounced on that mission too. "I read up on Napoleon in one of Amy's big books of history. But I can't make heads or tails of him."

"What do you want me to say?"

"Was Napoleon mainly a good thing or a bad thing for France? And for the other Western nations." Lester stretched out his arms and legs. "And could his empire work for us? You know, the conquests. Not the Waterloo part."

Gunner spread his arms and dropped the compress. "How the hell should I know? I write software, man. Ask Amy that question."

Lester grimaced. "Well, I would ask her, but she would just lecture me on not understanding history and tell me to read the stack of books she gave me. It's already hard enough to read through her birthday gift." He shifted on the cot. "Do you know that big history book has more than 1500 pages?"

"No shit." Gunner picked up the compress. "Really?"

"Yeah. I mean, it was your birthday gift too." Les tried to settle into the hard mattress. "Haven't you even flipped it open?"

"Are you kidding me? I use it to keep my hockey magazines from sliding off the shelf."

"Yeah, me too." Lester nodded. "So, you understand that if I'm going to be king, I won't have time for any heavy reading." Lester glanced at Gunner out of the corner of his eye. "I need a fast answer. Napoleon; good or bad?"

"Shit man, why do you even care?"

"Well, you know, Napoleon was an emperor. It could be the right career move for me."

Gunner groaned into the wall. "Les, your head is so far up your ass that I'm not going to be able to pull it out for you."

"Think about it, man. Maybe I should aim higher." Lester's eyelids drooped. "I mean, King Lester the Groovy is awesome, but maybe I can do better."

Gunner stood over him. "You're dead set on that name? Lester the Groovy? Not, 'the Great', or 'the Terrible', or something else?"

Lester closed his eyes, "Shit man, you've seen my moves on the dance floor. No one can touch me."

"Except for the big cop who gave you a black eye."

Lester's eyelids flicked open. "Fuck! I have a black eye?"

Gunner peered at Lester, "you're about halfway there, man. Trust me, hockey wisdom."

"Shit! I can't go to the disco with a black eye!" Lester put a hand through the lens-less frame. "How would it look to my subjects?"

"That's the least of your problems, man."

Lester blew out a ragged breath. "Maybe I can get the copper guillotined for it. You know, for high treason or something." He looked at Gunner. "What was that cop's name?"

"I don't remember, man." Gunner sighed. "And you can't go around chopping people's heads off just because you got a black eye. You started it, remember."

"Yeah, maybe the guillotine is a bit harsh. How about a whipping?" Lester cringed at Gunner's black look. "Anyway, Amy would know."

There was another long, plebeian silence in the cell as they listened to each other's slow breathing. Gunner leaned into the bars and cocked head. Lester could hear voices down the corridor but he couldn't make out a word of what was being said. He thought of his black eye in the middle of the disco dance floor and grimaced when he felt Gunner over him.

Gunner shook Lester's shoulder. "Did my dad really call me 'bourgeois'?"

"Nah. I made that part up." Lester stared at the upside-down face. "But he did call you a gamer."

"Shit, man!" Gunner kicked the cot's leg. "I studied computer science for four years!"

"Yeah, but your sister studied medicine for eight. And she has her own practice." Lester spread his hands. "Your dad's words. Sorry man."

"Fuck that!" Gunner paced across the cell. "I write software! How many people can do that?"

"I dunno." Lester cracked his neck. "If you look online, it seems like everyone can do it."

"Well, they can't!"

"Maybe you should shoot higher." Lester ruffled his shaggy mane. "Like me."

"Yeah, right. King."

"I meant duke. Unless you want to usurp my crown." Lester's head swooned as he turned to look at Gunner. "We can have a dance-off for it."

"Oh shit, Les." Gunner sank into the prison bars. "Please stop!"

"You'd lose anyway. You can't dethrone King Lester the Groovy."

Gunner stuck his face through the bars again and spoke to the universe. "I should have figured my sister was my dad's favourite."

"Yeah, I thought it was kind of obvious at your birthday." Lester tried to crane his neck. "How'd you guess?"

"Because he said so."

"Brilliant detective work, inspector Singh."

Gunner stormed over to Lester with flailing arms. "The first time my dad said it I thought he was joking!"

"And the second time?" Lester squinted with one eye.

"C'mon man, you know how my dad's always pullin' a fast one."

"Yeah, your dad can be pretty funny." Lester grinned. "Like when he mimicked the prime minister's speech at your birthday."

"Yeah, exactly!" Gunner put his hands in his pockets and dropped the compress. "Shit! Anyway, I can never tell when he's being serious."

"You can still make up for lost time and impress him."

"How?"

"By fulfilling your role as my faithful duke."

Gunner grabbed Lester's shirt. "Les, I swear I'm going to throttle you!"

"That would be bad news, dude. I can get you guillotined for high treason and you'll never become duke. They your sister will take over." Lester gave him an owlish stare. "What do you think of that?"

Gunner kicked his compress across the cell floor. "Les, man, you don't realize just how fucked we are."

"We'll see."

Chapter 12: The Man vs The King:

Heavy steps echoed outside of the cell and Gunner whispered to Lester harshly with a pained expression on his face. Gunner slid back to the far wall and motioned to Lester to stand. Lester crossed his arms and sank as deep as his wiggling shoulders would let him burrow into the hard mattress. Gunner shook his head and muttered as the keys jangled in the bars and the door creaked open to reveal the same two scowling officers from the King's Revolutionary Smoothie Flash Mob.

"Wrigglesworth, on your feet." The bigger of the two said.

Lester cocked an eyebrow and swung a leg over the edge. Then he slithered enough to lower the other leg until one foot nearly touched the ground. He heaved himself up to a sitting position with a grunt and steadied his weight on the edge of the cot. Slowly, he pushed himself upright and gave a big stretch as Gunner put his heads in his hands. Lester smiled at the stormy faced officers.

"Wrigglesworth, if you keep that up, I will drag you to the Right Honourable Fischer in cuffs." His tone was flat. "You know that, right?"

"I'm just a mild-mannered law clerk." Lester squinted. "Officer Webber."

Officer Webber looked at his colleague who shrugged. "You gonna give us any trouble this time, wise guy?"

"Nah."

"Do anything stupid and I'm going twist your arm until you scream and slap cuffs on you." Webber motioned for Lester to come forward. "You walk in front of me, Singh will walk with Officer Lopez. Is that clear for the both of you?"

"Yes, Officer Webber." Gunner shot Lester a look.

"Crystal," Lester said.

"Alright, then let's go."

Lester and Gunner walked down the neon lit hall with Webber and Lopez on their heels. They reached the double doors which were buzzed and opened automatically. They continued down another long hall and to a check point where they were run over with wands and walked through a metal detector while the officers waited impassively on the other side. They made their way down another short corridor until Webber ordered them to stop. He knocked on a door and entered, shutting it behind him. After a minute he returned and motioned for Lester and Gunner to walk inside the office.

"The Right Honourable Fischer has been kind enough to receive you both without handcuffs and without an officer present." Webber stared at Lester. "I expect you to behave impeccably."

Lester gestured to Gunner. "What about him?"

Webber's face contorted and from behind him Fischer spoke. "That's fine, Officer Webber. I've dealt with more foolish men than him." Fischer looked at Lester and Gunner. "I can see Mr. Singh is a sensible man. You can leave them with me."

"Yes sir." Webber leaned into Lester. "I'm going to be right outside that door, got it?"

"Got it." Lester turned towards Fischer before Webber had even reached the door and gave him a dazzling smile. "Good afternoon, Mr. Fischer."

"Mr. Wrigglesworth, you may refer to me as Justice Fischer."

"Is that what you dispense?"

Gunner grabbed his arm, "Les, shut up!"

Fisher shook his head. "Mr. Wrigglesworth, I would suggest you listen to Mr. Singh." He tapped a fountain pen on a leatherbound notepad. "The only reason why I agreed to this meeting is because my former colleague Eveyln Harper pleaded with me to do so." He gave them a cold stare. "Depending on how I want to examine the events of today, I can charge the both you with a long list of offences that will result in a prison sentence."

Lester strutted to Fischer's desk and plopped down on a comfy looking leather chair. "Why would you want to do that?"

"Mr. Wrigglesworth, I didn't invite you to sit."

Lester ran his hand over the leather and whispered, "smooth as a law clerk's skin."

"I heard that, Mr. Wrigglesworth." Fischer said. "If you think your treatment is unfair then you have no understanding of the seriousness of your crimes."

"Since when is revolution a crime?"

Fischer raised an eyebrow. "Is that what you call your foolish charade in a private place of work with a mob of people?" Fischer tapped his fountain pen. "And what would you say about assaulting two police officers?

"Hang on there, Justice Fischer." Gunner said. "The police officers started it. We were just talking when they threatened us."

"Mr Singh, it is against the law to assault a police officer."

"Yeah, we know." Gunner swallowed hard. "But, they were really aggressive and we panicked."

"Fischer," Lester leaned back and snuggled into the plump backing. "That's a German last name, isn't it?"

"Mr. Wrigglesworth, I believe it's time that –"

"You don't descend from the House of Hanover, by any chance?"

"Les!" Gunner's eyes popped. "Would you shut up?"

Fischer's eyes turned hard. "Young man, I'm not in the mood for games."

"Nah," Lester said. "I didn't think so."

Lester nearly poked himself in the eye through the missing lens and frowned, thinking of the justice to come. "Do you use Blather, Justice Fischer?"

"It seems that we cannot understand each other, Mr. Wrigglesworth. Therefore I – Where are you going?" Fischer pounded his palm on the desk. "Don' you dare walk away and turn your back on me!"

Lester stood at the window that looked down on the courthouse square below. "There's an interesting feature that I didn't know about. You know you can use a delay timer to send out messages and organize events?" Lester looked at Fischer from out of the corner of his three eyes. "Of course, you can never be sure how many people will actually show up. But I suppose for the right cause,—like wrongly arresting the King of Blunt City—people might want to participate in significant numbers." Lester clasped his hands behind his back and thrust out his chin. "Against acts of high treason, you can get quite a turnout."

Fischer cocked an ear and stood up abruptly. "What is all of that racket?"

Lester smiled. "That, Justice Fischer, is the King's Revolutionary Smoothie pounding on you're your door."

Gunner sprinted to the window and skidded to a stop. "Les, my man!" He thumped his hands on the glass and stared down at the sea of people below. "You are absolutely insane!"

***** End *****

ENRICO PICCHI

THE CAPTAIN STOOD OVER THE TREE

The Blunt City Chronicles

The Blunt City Chronicles: The Captain Stood Over the Tree:

The white electricians truck rolled up to the Northwest corner of Captain Blunt Plaza and stopped in a tow away zone a short distance from the malfunctioning city streetlamp. From the driver's side William Mason hopped down and shut the door almost before touching the asphalt. His dark eyes cast a gaze across the hood to watch at his partner, Nathan Adamski struggle to push himself out of his seat and thud to the pavement. Bill tied back his hair, shut and locked the door and put the keys in his pocket. He adjusted his blue work jacket on his skinny frame and narrowed his gaze as he looked at the city square. He ignored the wave from Nate and walked onto the plaza and away from the streetlamp they had been called to repair.

He stopped at the foot of the nearest statue and crossed his arms. Bill's eyes went from the twisted First Nations sculpture to the enormous monolith that extolled Captain Blunt. He tapped his chin as he scrutinized the First Nations casting. The people of Blunt City called it the 'totem pole statue,' but it certainly wasn't a totem pole, and not because of its insignificant height. Bill circled the sculptured and hazarded a guess. A spruce tree with an eagle perched on top. But what was at the foot of the sculpture was anybody's guess.

"Bill, you gonna help me or not?" Nate wheezed as he pulled the tool cart out of the back of the van.

"It's your turn to unload the truck, Nate." Bill watched his obese partner lumber towards the streetlamp. "I took care of it on our first call."

Nate glared as he huffed towards the lamp. "You're not helping me because I'm fat."

Bill grinned. "Damn straight, butterball. It was your stupid idea to trade off unloading the truck anyway."

Bill chuckled as Nate cursed and made the return trip to fetch the extension ladder for the emergency repair. It was a fine day, spoiled only by the Sunday emergency service that Juice Electrical Company provided to Blunt City. Bill thought it was ridiculous to call it an Emergency Service. Being on-call on Sundays meant working more hours than on any given Monday. Bill signed up often for the overtime pay, but today he would have rather been sitting on a park bench feeding the birds with his family.

“C’mon, Bill.” Nate panted. “I’ve got everything unloaded. At least help me set up.”

“You should be thankful I’m here.” Bill said. “I’m the one who’s going to climb up the ladder.”

“Yeah, yeah, get your skinny ass over here,” Nate grumbled.

Bill gave one last look at the First Nations corkscrew tree cowering in the shadow of the soaring Captain Blunt and sauntered over to Nate. “Alright, the call notes state the problem isn’t the bulb.”

“No,” Nate said. “They changed it out yesterday and the lamp didn’t come on.”

“Then why didn’t they troubleshoot the problem?” Bill scowled. “Who was on call yesterday?”

Nate grinned. “Matt and Joris.”

“Shit.” Bill said as he rummaged through their tool kit. “Why does JEC keep putting those two clowns together?”

“I don’t know, man.” Nate smirked. “To give us the overtime work.”

“Yeah, but someone has to pay for that overtime.”

“Right,” Nate winked. “Blunt City.”

Bill shook his head. “Our city tax dollars, hard at work.”

“You ready to clamber up there?” Nate fastened on the safety belt to the lamppost. “Ladder’s ready.”

Bill curled his lip. “I can see you respected the four to one rule.”

Nate pointed over Bill’s head. “If I did that, the base of the ladder would be over by the statue.”

“Which statue?”

“The totem pole.”

Bill folded his arms. "It's not a totem pole."

Nate groaned. "Don't get all high and mighty on me Bill." He looked at his watch. "I wanna be done by noon so we can have greasy lunch over at The Burnt Toast."

Bill looked at Nate's ample belly. "You gonna order a salad?"

"Yeah, I'm gonna order a fucking salad." He smacked his lips. "I'm getting' steak and eggs with a side order of hashbrowns. What about you?"

"A salad."

Nate laughed. "Yeah right. You're gonna get steak too. With butter garlic mashed potatoes 'cause you don't get fat."

Bill grinned. "Maybe." He looked up at the lamppost. "Luckily, it's a low one. When I fall, I probably won't break my neck."

"Shut-up, man." Nate laughed. "The ladder's harnessed. Now get your bony ass up there."

"Sure thing, Hardy."

Nate punched him in the arm. "I wish I were that skinny. Now get climbing."

Bill checked his toolbelt, fitted his helmet and climbed up the lamppost. He secured himself to the eyebolt and opened the lamp covering. He removed the bulb, looked at the socket for signs of a flash burn and began test with his multimeter. He frowned and muttered under his breath. He removed the capacitor and waved it in the air and heard Nate grunt below. Bill rolled his eyes and changed out the burnt capacitor then fitted the bulb in place and bolted the covering back in place. He unlatched his safety hook and slithered down the ladder.

"Wow," He rolled his eyes. "Real head-scratcher of a job."

Nate wheezed out a laugh. "Don't worry man, Matt and Joris are gonna get reamed for this fuck-up."

"They better get shit for this one." Bill said. "Hopefully it will end the escapades of the comic duo."

Nate snorted. "I'll call the city and tell them they can power the lamp back up."

Nate took the company cell phone out of his pocket and dialed while Bill drifted across the plaza. He looked at the stern Captain Blunt, his right arm cradling a globe, his left arm held high as it clutched a flag. The mighty Captain stood in the central, northern section of the plaza. Raised up on a massive granite pedestal, the intrepid seafaring conqueror presided over the downtown. To the right of the statute was the cryptic, twisted tube of metal that somehow represented all the other Nations that had been there before him. Bill looked from statue to statue when he felt a nudge.

"The light's been tested." Nate pointed behind them. "I'll call them back and tell them they can set the sunset timer."

Bill looked up. "Yeah, great." He turned back to the statues. "Nate, what do you make of the statues?"

Nate swiveled his head. "You mean Captain Blunt standing over the totem pole?"

"That's a good way of putting it." Bill's sneered at the massive Captain Blunt. "It's rather difficult to miss the message, don't you think?"

A flat line formed over Nate's blubbery face. "You're always pissed off 'cause you're a wronged *Injun*." Nate scanned Bill's stormy face and flushed. "Sorry, Bill. I was only joking, man."

"What if I were to say that you *Polacks* gave up to Hitler without hardly even a fight?"

"I don't know," Nate shrugged. "Only my grandfather was Polish." He cocked an eyebrow. "Really? They gave up without fighting?"

"No, not really." Bill sighed. "Just forget it man."

Nate put a hand on his shoulder. "C'mon Bill. I didn't mean anything by it."

Bill gave him a crooked smile. "I know, Nate." He sighed. "But sometimes you're an ass."

Nate voice oozed buttery enthusiasm. "C'mon man, it's past noon. Let's pack up the van and then get some grease into us. At 1:30pm we have to make our next call over at the Covenant Tower." He nudged Bill. "Grease, Billy-Bob?"

Bill laughed. "Alright, Nate. Let's pack up."

Bill unfasted the ladder as Nate repacked their tools. Bill handed Nate the keys to open the van as Bill pulled down the ladder and collapsed it into a moderately long two meters. Bill hoisted the ladder and together with Nate they secured it on the van top and locked up the van as the plaza filled up with an odd bunch of youngsters.

Nate pointed. "What is that, '60s cosplay?"

Bill looked at the growing sea of laughing twentysomethings. "I guess. But I think it's 70s cosplay."

Nate. "Yeah, I think you're right." Nate turned. "Geez, over by the trees there's a shitload more. And they're all walking over to Captain Blunt."

"Yeah, I think they're walking over to that skinny guy with the bushy hair." Bill started. "Jesus, he's as quick as a jack rabbit." He turned to Nate. "Did you see him hop the fence?"

"Yeah, and now he's up on the statue's pedestal." Nate's eyes widened as the music blared. "I know what this is! The kids have put together a flash mob!"

Bill smiled. "And a big one! There are hundreds of people here."

Nate pulled him back. "Let's get out of the way before they trample us."

The two stepped back as the crowd hollered and began dancing in unison. Bill and Nate watched from the sidelines as other onlookers stopped and pointed to the massive crown in Captain Blunt Plaza. Bill gaped at the throngs of people that kept perfect time as the skinny, dancing youth led them through a series of steps he couldn't name. He found himself bobbing to the music when the dancing stopped and the crowd cheered.

"C'mon Bill, stop gawking." He grabbed his sleeve. "Let's get over to The Burnt Toast before it fills up. I don't want to hurry lunch."

"With the way you eat every lunch is a hurry."

Nate laughed as he lumbered towards the diner. The two skirted the edge of the jubilant crown and stopped at the crosswalk. When the light turned in their favour, the ponderous Nate hurried across and made straight for The Burnt Toast. He pushed open the door with Bill on his heels and tramped up to the hostess. Nate pumped his fist when he heard 'last table over there' and he ambled towards a small table for two in the middle of the diner. Nate plopped down, grabbed the menu and waved it frantically until a waitress walked over to their table.

The waitress smiled. "Can I start you off with coffee?"

"Sure," Nate smiled. "But we're ready to order, too."

She laughed. "Sure, let's start with the coffees."

"For me a triple triple."

Bill raised an eyebrow at Nate then turned to the waitress. "Just a black coffee, thanks."

"And your orders?" She asked.

Nate grinned. "I'll have steak and eggs with a side of hashbrowns and buttered toast."

Bill shook his head. "I'll have steak and garlic mashed potatoes."

"Great!" The waitress's fingers tapped on her tablet. "I'll be back in a minute with your coffees."

Bill watched her leave and turned to Nate. "A triple triple? And you tack on buttered toast to your order?"

"Give me a break, Bill." Nate adjusted his enormous weight to a disapproving creak from his chair. "It's Sunday."

"You eat like every day was a Sunday."

Nate laughed. "Yeah, but today is Sunday for real." He gazed across the room. "I'm ordering desert, too."

"Nate, how the hell are you ever going to lose weight if you keep this up?"

"C'mon Bill, they have cherry pie on the menu!"

"When did you have time to look at the menu?"

"It's written on the blackboard behind you."

The server arrived with two steaming mugs, one black and the other cream. Bill blew on his and put it to his lips and sipped cautiously. "You'll be dead by forty."

"Maybe," Nate chortled. "But it will be with a mouthful of sweet, cherry pie."

Bill choked on his coffee as Nate laughed and slapped the table. "Shit man, I got you there!"

Bill coughed and grinned. "I'm gonna miss you when you're dead."

"Don't worry, Bill. I promise you'll see me again." Nate lip quivered as his eyes gleamed. "When Matt and Joris tie off your ladder they're gonna send you to an early grave!"

Bill and Nate howled with laughter, nearly spilling their mugs. Bill bent over at the waist and struck his head on the side of the table and Nate whooped out a laugh as the confused patrons turned to smirk at the scene. Bill rubbed his head with tears streaming down his face and Nate struggled to choke down his laughter. Their bewildered waitress stood next to their table with overloaded plates.

"Are you guys ok?" She looked back and forth at the two red faced men.

"Sorry, sorry," Bill wiped his eyes. "We've worked too many hours this week. We're just giddy. I promise, we're not drunk."

She giggled. "No problem, I know what you mean! Enjoy your lunch!"

The waitress set down their plates and turned to walk to a nearby booth that called out. Bill reached for his fork and knife, but hiccupped, sending Nate into gales of laughter. Bill put a fist into his mashed potatoes and Nate howled harder, triggering the neighbouring tables into laughter. The two settled into quiet giggles as they sucked in air and looked at each other. Bill wiped the mashed potatoes off his hand with a napkin.

"Stop it, Nate." Bill bit down on his lip. "You're gonna make me stab myself with my steak knife."

"Sorry, Bill." Nate wheezed. "I just keep seeing you up on an untied ladder with Matt and Joris below you on their smart phones." He giggled. "Messaging each other on Blather!"

"Enough, Nate." Bill waved his hand and took a huge breath. "Let's eat before our food gets cold."

The two settled cut their steaks with grinning faces. Bill ate methodically and smirked at the voracious Nate who gobbled down his food as though it were his last meal. Swigs of coffee interspersed their chewing to help wash down the grease. Before Bill had finished his last bite, Nate had already waved down the waitress to order himself a slice of cherry pie with ice-cream.

"You sure you don't want one?" Nate asked. "It's Sunday."

"I'm good, man." Bill said. "I'll just have another coffee."

Nate shrugged his blubbery shoulders. "Suit yourself." He looked at Bill and flushed. "So, about before ..."

Bill waved his hand. "Not again, Nate! They're gonna throw us out if we keep making a scene."

"No, not about Matt and Joris," Nate shifted. "I mean about the totem pole."

Bill gave him a flat look. "It's not a totem pole. We're in Ontario, Nate."

"Yeah, sorry." Nate lowered his eyes. "I didn't mean to call you an *Injun*. I was only trying to joke around. You know how I am."

"Don't worry about it." Bill flicked his fingers. "I'm not offended."

"You sure, Bill? Cause you looked pretty pissed when I said it."

"It was just bad timing." Bill sighed. "I was trying to figure out what the First Nations sculpture was. There's a plaque, but it only gives the artist's name and the sculpture name, but it doesn't say wat it is." Bill grimaced. "The sculpture is called 'Born Free.' Can you believe it?"

"Yeah, I can understand how that would irritate you." Nate squirmed around on his seat as he looked at Bill.

"Ok Nate, fire away." Bill said. "I know you want to ask me about being a Native. You've been dancing around it for the past few months. Pretty much since we started being paired up."

"Sorry Bill, I just don't know any other Natives."

"And I don't know any other Poles."

Nate chuckled. "Only my grandfather was pure blooded. Everyone else in my family is mixed." He gave Bill a lopsided grin. "You lived on the First Nations Reserve until you started working for JEC."

"Yeah, that's right. I was born and raised there."

"What was it like?"

"It was often a struggle. I didn't really notice it when I was really young and going to primary school. But once I got older and started going outside of the community, I really saw the difference."

"Like what?"

"The houses. You can totally see the difference compared to a regular neighbourhood." Bill picked up his mug. "The shops, too. There aren't any big chain stores, which is a good thing, but half the shops are trailers or rickety, wooden buildings. There aren't that many brick-and-mortar shops."

Nate nodded. "Gotcha. So, kind of a shitty environment."

"The homes and commercial stuff, yeah." Bill said. "But it's not bad like the Reserves way up North."

Nate hunched his shoulders. "That's where they have the drug problems, right?"

Bill sipped his coffee. "Yeah. We have it on our Reserve too, but at least we don't have the gangs and drug dealers scaring the shit out of people."

"Why did you move away?"

"For work, Nate." Bill sighed. "I mean, I had work on the Reserve as an electrician through a local company, but the pay was shit." He gave him a sour smile. "And I had too many requests for freebies. I needed a fresh start so I took a job with JEC and moved to Blunt City."

Nate grinned. "Where all your extra earnings are going to rent."

Bill laughed. "Just about. The overtime pay is good, so if I keep up the extra hours, I'll make a tidy bundle when I'm done."

"Then what?" Nate asked. "Do you think you'll move back to the reserve?"

"I really don't know, Nate." Bill gulped his coffee. "My wife and kid are there, but I don't know if I want to go back. Maybe I'll bring them to the city."

Nate's eyes lit up as the waitress set a huge portion of cherry pie and ice-cream in front of him. "You sure you don't want a bite?" Nate sliced off a huge chunk and stuffed it in his mouth.

Bill watched him with a half-smile. "I'm good."

"So," Nate mumbled through his cherry pie. "I mean, be honest. Don't you think it was a good thing that Captain Blunt discovered Canada?"

"Discovered it?" Bill frowned. "You mean the Natives living here didn't know where they were?"

"You know what I mean." Nate plunged his fork into the orange sized ice-cream ball. "I mean, life was way harder back then."

"Maybe it was."

"I mean, look at all the technology you guys have now."

"We all have that technology."

Nate rolled his eyes. "C'mon Bill, I'm not being an ass. I'm asking serious questions."

"Sorry Nate, you're right." Bill sighed and squared his shoulders. "So let me answer you seriously. I don't know what would have been better or worse. I was born in the early 1990s like you. What I do know is that the government of Ontario didn't respect the original contracts and the Reserve is one tenth the size what was promised."

"So, you can't hunt on the Reserve?"

"It's not about hunting, Nate." Bill frowned. "It's about conquest and false promises. No one owned the land, it was used by all the tribes. Maybe there were conflicts, but they had their own ways of solving their problems." Bill tinkered with his mug. "Now a bunch of people own the land. But the part that should have gone to a community is in private hands."

Nate scooped a blob of ice cream off the table. "You told me the Reserve is fighting for the land in the courts."

"Yeah, but it's a hopeless case. We all know that." Bill shook his head. "The Committee is just fighting in the hopes of getting some kind of monetary compensation. But there's no way the Reserve will get the land back." He looked down at his mug. "If the Committee got the land back, then what? Knock down the homes and businesses that have been there for generations and displace hundreds of thousands of non-native people?"

"No, I guess not." Nate licked his fork. "It's a pretty shitty situation."

"Yeah." Bill said. "It is."

Bill waved down the waitress for more coffee as the two sat in a melancholy silence. The waitress came over and smiled as she filled their mugs and left cream and sugar on the table. Nate poured in shot after shot of as Bill warmed his hands on his mug. The big man mixed his sugary delight and smiled. He took out his smartphone and typed out a message on Blather and slid his phone across the table. Bill laughed at the thank-you note to Matt and Joris and shook his head at the grinning Nate. The two clinked their mugs just as Bill thought of his young son. He was going to give him a good life, he was sure of it. There might be a few years of belt tightening, but he would give his family the future they deserved. To hell with the captain standing over the tree.

The Blunt City Chronicles:
New Beginnings:

Inside the Covenant Tower atrium all was quiet except for the noise of the industrial floor scrubber on the tiles. Sunday was a slow day with rarely a visitor except for the cleaners and the odd repair man. George Wendel didn't normally like to pick up the Sunday shift, but with his first child on the way he and Linda had decided it would be best that he work as much overtime as he could before their lives were turned upside down. They were excited, but concerned with covering the mortgage on their house only on his salary. For the first year Linda had decided to stay at home, and if possible, only work part time after that. George wasn't sure it was a good idea on his meagre salary and grimaced at the thought of working seven days a week to cover the bills. But he didn't want to argue with Linda and would hug her close and say they would figure it out.

George smiled at the cleaner that slowly moved past him in one of the many rounds that would be needed to clean the immense floor. His eyes followed the elderly man dressed in a way that he couldn't identify. It seemed like exotic dress for a place of business. George turned back to the monitors that watched over the many nooks and crannies in Covenant Tower. The building was nearly empty, with painters on floor fourteen and office cleaners working their way down from the top to the bottom. It would likely make for a long, dull day.

With a big sigh George picked up a pen and scribbled out a drawing. George hadn't planned on being a security guard and he certainly didn't want to make it his life career. He had studied community health services, and had worked in the field for two years, but found the work too stressful and the pay too low. He couldn't reconcile his job as a geriatric care worker when he experienced the coldness of the company administrators. He didn't know if all centres were the same, but he decided not to find and started to look for other work. He got lucky when a neighbour had suggested him to Covenant Towers as a night guard, and after a quick crash course he was hired. A few weeks into the job a staff member quit and he was moved to the dayshift which meant he didn't have premium hourly pay but could manage his life better with Linda. That had been three years ago and though he promised he would attend night classes to study something that could give him better pay he never got around to it. He never dared think about his true passion, drawing comic books. It was an impossible dream and he extinguished the thought any time it entered his mind.

George continued to scribble out a muscular figure in a cape. He put down his pen and put the superhero out of his mind as he gazed across the atrium. He didn't realize he was staring until the cleaner stopped and smiled. "Hello sir. Do you need something?"

George flushed. "Ah, no. Sorry." He tried to place the accent. "Um, everything's going well? You'll finish on time?"

The gentlemen smiled. "Yes, it's a big floor, but I can get it done before 4pm."

"Great. Perfect." George looked him up and down and wondered if he was Indian.

"Do you have any questions?" the elderly man tilted his head and smiled with his eyes.

"Ah, no." George stammered. "Why do you ask?"

"Because you keep looking at my shalwar kameez."

"Your what?"

The man chuckled. "My shirt and trousers. It is traditional Pakistani dress."

"Oh, that's where you from." George flushed, "Not that it matters."

The gentleman laughed again. "It's fine. I know my dress is not common in the business district." He held his hand over the security counter. "My name is Latif. Latif Khan."

"Nice to meet you, Mr. Khan." George stood and grabbed his hand. "My name is George Wendel."

"Please, call me Latif."

"Sure, ok." George hesitated. "Latif. So, have you been in Canada long?"

"Oh, about thirty years now." Latif said.

"Wow, longer than I've been alive!" George grinned then bit his lip. "Sorry, I didn't mean any disrespect."

Latif waved his hand. "It's not a problem, I know I'm well-seasoned."

Georged shrugged. "So, do you miss Pakistan?"

"Some things I do." Latif smiled "I came over when I was just a little bit older than you are now, so I'm trapped between two worlds."

"Yeah, I guess so." George said. "I've never been outside of Canada. Well, except for the US. You know, like, New York, Los Angeles and Las Vegas."

"Those are interesting places" Latif said. "Many people look for their hopes and dreams there."

"Yeah, I guess." George tried to puzzle out what he meant. He picked up his pen and unconsciously began to scribble. "Why did you come? If you don't mind me asking."

"I thought I could help here." Latif dark eyes looked up and then back at George. "Perhaps inspire someone to achieve his dreams."

"Oh, yeah. I guess that's why most people come over." George said. "So, uh, Latif. What did you do in Pakistan?"

"For a time I was a doctor."

"What?" George clamped his hand over his mouth. "Sorry, that was rude. I just, well ..."

Latif offered him a thumb's up. "That's fine, I understand it's not what you would expect from a man cleaning an office building."

"No, no it's not." George put his hand under his chin and frowned. "Why aren't you a doctor now?"

"My degree was not recognized." Latif said. "It would have required additional studies before I could practice in Blunt City. But it's no matter as I found many other ways to assist good hearted people."

"Oh, well that's good." George shrugged and searched his mind for a less personal topic. "So, is it hot all the time in Pakistan?"

Latif laughed softly. "Certainly not in the Kaghan Valley."

"I guess that's where you are from?" George looked at his monitor and pressed a button.

Latif nodded. "Yes, it's in the Northwest."

"Then it's cold like in Blunt City?"

"Not always," Latif said. "The climate in the mountains is very unpredictable."

"Excuse me, Latif." George waved to an odd couple that approached the desk with a ladder and tool bags. One was a very thin man with long hair and his obese partner made George look skinny. He thought they reminded him of some famous people, but he could not think of who. "Good afternoon. You're the electricians, right?"

"Yeah, we're from JEC," the skinny man replied. "We got an emergency call that the tenth floor has lost all its socket power on one wall."

"Exactly." George handed them a tablet. "Just put your company name and signatures there." He handed them badges as they signed with their fingers. "Please remember to bring back the badges and sign out."

The skinny man nodded. "Sure thing. We'll let you know if it's going to be a long job." The skinny man picked up the ladder and walked with his partner to the elevators.

George turned back to the cleaner. "Sorry Latif, what were we saying?"

Latif started to walk back to the scrubber. "George, I don't want to distract you and I really should get moving if I want to finish before 4pm."

"You're right but let's just talk for another minute." George thought he might never get another chance to learn about Pakistan. "What's it like in, uh? Where again are you from in Pakistan?"

"Khyber Pakhtunkhwa Kaghan Wadi."

George widened his eyes. "Where?"

Latif laughed. "I gave you the entire province name and the Kaghan Valley in Hindko." Latif's eyes became unfocused. "I lived in the mountains, a beautiful but difficult place. It is a land of summer fairy tales but also of dangerously harsh winters." He shook his head. "In the winter snow and ice often blocked the roads completely."

"Wow." George said. "It must have been hard to get around."

Latif nodded. "It was, especially when I travelled the community as a doctor, and I absolutely needed to arrive in the remote villages. I was young and energetic, but winter emergencies were difficult to manage. Sometimes impossible."

George leaned back in his chair. "Yeah, I guess it would have been." He scratched his head. "What did you mean that the mountains were a place of fairy tales?"

Latif stood very still for a moment, then he raised his wrist and squinted. "I would like to continue but it's getting late." His eyes twinkled. "Are you sure?"

"Just one fairy tale." George pleaded. "I've got my first kid on the way, and it would be nice to learn some."

Latif offered George a small smile under his thick moustache. "Very well, then. Let me tell you a story of the jinn of Mount Tirich Mir." He clasped his hands behind his back and bowed his head. George watched him inhale deeply. "I was only a boy, ten going on eleven, when my family took a trip to visit Chitral at the Mount Tirich Mir. Climbing to the top of the mountain was impossible, at it is more than seven thousand seven hundred meters tall, but the view of the mountain from Chitral is breath-taking."

"Yeah," George nodded. "It must be awesome. It's pretty flat here in the Greater Blunt City area."

Latif continued as though he had not heard. "Tirich Mir is a place of wonder, unlike any place in the world." He smiled broadly with a playful look in his eyes. "It's a land of magical creatures, with the likes of fairies and jinn."

"Fairies, huh?" George crossed his arms. "You mean make-believe stuff. There's no such thing as fairies."

"Perhaps it is as you say," Latif said with a mischievous smile. "But let me tell you my story about the jinn and you can decide for yourself."

"Gin? Like the drink?"

Latif chuckled, "No, jinn are known in the West as genie."

"Like in the bottle?" George asked.

"Not in this case, they are the same type of creature." Latif gave him a curious stare before he spoke. "I would like to help you, George. Would you like to hear my story?"

"Absolutely! Please."

Latif nodded. "It was summer when my father took us for a vacation in Chitral. Though the city is high in the valley, in the summer months it is quite warm during the day with a cool, dry breeze. For families it is a wonderful place where children can run freely, splash in the icy river or nap in a sloping field. Parents can keep an eye on the little ones easily, so my younger siblings could wander around on the lush grass.

"The day before our father had taken us to visit the Chitral Fort, and being a young boy, I imagined myself as a soldier, armed with a sword and fighting off enemies who dared to besiege us." Latif shook his head. "Foolish fancies of a boy, but I could occupy my mind all day with my own invented stories. I can remember very well running up and down the stairs, slashing with my wooden scimitar. There were cannons inside the fort, and I ordered my imaginary soldiers to fire them at our enemies. Inside Chitral Fort was a gold and white hall. There I remember pretending to marry a princess that I promised I would defend to my last breath." He grinned. "Such foolishness of youth."

"I did the same stuff," George said. "Except I used to pretend I scored the winning goal for The Blunt City Conquerors and lifted the Stanley Cup."

"Boys will be boys no matter where they are from." Latif gave George a strange look. "We are all dreamers looking for a new beginning."

George tapped his chin. "Yeah, I guess we are." He shook his head. "What about the jinn?"

"Ah yes! My father took us hiking at the foot of Tirich Mir and we stopped for a picnic." Latif mimed sleep. "We were all very tired, so we laid down on our mats and blankets to rest under the warm sun and cool breeze. I was the oldest and full of energy, so I decided to walk about while my family slept. I rounded a bend in the path and found a large bush with strange, heart-shaped fruits on them. I walked up to the bush and admired it's dark and spikey foliage and strange berries. It was only when I reached out to take a blood-red fruit that I noticed a large blue-green serpent coiled up next to the bush."

George started. "You mean a snake?"

"Yes. And a very large one." Latif mimed the terrifying dimensions. "I had seen a few species of serpents, or snakes, in my young years, but nothing like this one. Apart from its enormous size, the bluish green scales and orange eyes were like unlike anything I had ever seen before. The snake watched me placidly, more poised than coiled. As though it were waiting for me."

George frowned. "Waiting? You mean it wanted to eat you?"

Latif smiled. "No, nothing of the sort. The snake simply watched me calmly, it's tongue flickering and its orange eyes unblinking. Other than its tongue it was perfectly still. Then slowly, very slowly it began to uncoil part of its body, the part with its head, and it raised itself upwards until it could look down upon me."

George widened his eyes. "Geez! That sounds scary!"

"Other than being startled when it first rose, I felt no fear." Latif put an elbow on his hand, bent his wrist and mimed a snake wavering back and forth. "The snake looked at me with its unblinking eyes and then a thought appeared in my mind. Suddenly, at not yet eleven years of age I asked myself, *what do I want from this life*?"

"Really? A snake was staring at you, and you asked yourself what you want to be when you grow up?" George scratched his cheek. "I don't want to doubt you, but that's kinda weird, Latif. I would have high-tailed it outta there."

"Listening to myself speak these words, I can understand your sentiment." Latif said as he lowered his arms. "But I assure you I felt no fear and the thought suddenly appeared. It was a very strong thought. In that instant, it completely consumed me and I could think of nothing else."

"Really? That's a weird thought for a kid?" George asked. "What did you do?"

"For a time, I did nothing at all. Then a second thought entered my mind." Latif said. "I thought, *what am I willing to do to achieve my goal*? This thought was even stronger than the first. So strong in fact that for an instant I felt my head swim and nearly tripped over my own feet."

"Did the snake bite you." George but two fingers on his wrist. "Maybe it was poison."

"No, the snake did not bite me. Most definitely not. It still hadn't moved." Latif once again mimed the snake. "It was extended above me, but it did not strike. It was perfectly still. Then, as it stared at me, I had another strong thought."

"What was it?"

"*Help the worthy ones*." Though Latif's voice was barely a whisper, it chimed in the empty atrium. "This is the best translation I can give you from my thoughts in Hindko." His features were relaxed but serious. "I knew that I had to seek out people in need. Even those who thought they didn't need help. I knew I had to find them and assist them."

George turned the thought in his mind. It wasn't too far from what he had done. "You know Latif, I think I helped people too. I'm not sure if they were worthy, but I helped people in senior care homes." George bobbed back and forth in his chair several times as a thought began to form. "You know what, Latif? The seniors were worthy of my help."

Latif's eyes twinkled as he smiled. "Yes George, they were."

George sighed. "But I stopped helping them because the pay was terrible."

"Was that really why you stopped?" Latif stood completely still, except for the fingers of his hand which formed a wave.

George looked up at the older man's serene gaze. "Well, not exactly. I didn't like the management. They only cared about making sure things were done by the book. But when you have old people with no family, sometimes you need to throw the rule book out the window and just sit with them." George felt himself flush. "Sorry, that doesn't sound very professional."

"It sounds caring."

George saw the atrium light filter around Latif. The dust swirled and danced and flickered like tens of thousands of stars. "Yeah. I did care about them. I really did."

"I know George." The atrium light intensified around Latif. "You are a good man and I think it's time you did something for yourself."

"What do you mean?"

"It's time to follow your dreams, George." The light poured through the glass and George had to avert his gaze as he listened to the old man speak. "You are worthy. It's time to pick up your pen again and return to drawing."

George put a hand up to shield his eyes. "How did you know about my comic books?"

"We're done, man." A voice floated from across the hall.

"What? One second, Latif." George blinked furiously as he swivelled and slowly focused his gaze on the approaching electricians. "Oh, it's you two. You're done already?"

The skinny electrician handed him the badges. "Yeah, we got all but one of the sockets on the wall to work."

"How'd you get it done so quick?" George asked.

"A damaged socket that caught my eye as soon as I walked in the office. I jumpered it to get the others along the corridor to work. But you'll need to order a replacement for the damaged one." He signed the tablet. "I covered it over so you can tell the law firm that the socket with the red tape is unwired."

"Perfect. I'll tell maintenance to order a new one." George threw the badges in a large bowl and looked past the electricians. He frowned and peeked around them. George stood and widened his eyes. "Hey, did you guys see where Latif went?"

The skinny electrician cocked an eyebrow. "Who?"

"The elderly gentleman. The cleaner with the robe-like clothes." George tapped the counter. "He was standing right here when you first came in and when you came back down now."

The two electricians looked at each other and shrugged. "Sorry, man. We didn't see anyone."

George looked at the two electricians for a moment then turned his head to observe the atrium. He looked at the monitors but saw no sign of Latif nor his cleaning machine. Latif might have quickly left the building without him noticing, but how did he manage to move the rider-scrubber so quickly? The slow-moving unit must have weighed five hundred pounds. "Uh, never mind. Thanks, and have a good day."

"Yeah, you too." The electricians picked up their gear and walked to the front doors. George watched them intently. The skinny one had a poking gate, the fat one lumbered clumsily beside him.

George scratched his head. He would watch the security films as soon as his shift finished to understand how Latif had left so quickly.

He was disappointed, he had enjoyed talking to the man and still had a lot of questions about his homeland. He also wanted to understand how Latif knew he used to draw comic books. He was certain he hadn't said anything, and Latif didn't seem like the kind of man who would be on Blather looking at the social pages.

There was a prismatic whirl of light on the desk. George blinked at the multicoloured drawing pen that rested next to the sign-in tablet. He reached over and picked it up. It was well weighted and seemed to be of excellent quality. He uncapped the pen and looked at the jet-black nib. George took a piece of paper out and slowly began to draw across the page. The pen glided effortlessly and in a few minutes he had drawn a gorgeous snake next to a large bush with heart shaped fruit. He picked up the sheet and admired his drawing. He put the pen back down to the paper and wrote with calligraphy that matched anything he had seen written by the masters. George grinned as he held up the sheet again and whispered *new beginnings*.

ENRICO PICCHI

BLUNT CITY AFTER MIDNIGHT

The Blunt City Chronicles

The Blunt City Chronicles Volume I:
Blunt City After Midnight:

The metal door groaned open to a bleachy smell that made Sally Chu wince. The pungent scent was not a good sign. The acidic odour reeked of damaged film and the bleach suggested a hasty attempt of cleaning up the environment before she arrived to begin the search. Sally knew that this was the 'forgotten' wing of the Blunt City Archives, but the stinging smell made her think that it had been completely abandoned until yesterday. Her wince seemed to have caught the attention of Blunt City Film Registry archivist Joseph Kalda as he mumbled something, gave an embarrassed shrug and turned on the lights.

The neon lamps buzzed to life to reveal a long corridor lined by evenly spaced metal shelves. The shelves held countless film reels stacked so haphazardly that the sight made Sally grimace. The Blunt City Film Registry was the most important archive in Canada, and second in North America only to National Film Registry in the Unites States. Sally had been in the new wing which was pristine and marshal in its structure. Staring at the narrow, dingy hall of the old wing made her stomach clench. Though she still thought it was possible to unearth a rare film reel, the complete neglect drastically reduced the likelihood it would play in a projector.

Sally was looking for an orphan film, one that might have been forgotten forever if not for a television commercial nearly twenty years ago that featured a clip of the 1927 silent horror mystery film entitled *Blunt City After Midnight*. The brief clip was of the killer, a man possessed by a demon who wore a cape, top hat and sneered with razor-sharp teeth. The laughable horror clip of the assassin gnashing and clawing frantically had set off a rage with teenagers desperate to watch the silent film. Short clips of teens filming themselves mimicking the scene had made the rounds on Blather, the first ever success for the then nascent social network.

When the commercial came out featuring the clip, Sally had been one of those teens enraptured by the ridiculously old-style horror and badly wanted to see the film with her friends. She remembered trying to download it, but all the renamed files were either kids' movies or creepy porn videos. None of her friends had any luck until through someone's cousin the film was found. But the problem was that it was incomplete, with parts too grainy to make out and twelve minutes completely missing. The novelty of the film wore off and for years she had forgotten about *Blunt City After Midnight*. But it had in part ignited her desire to study the technical side of film.

At Blunt City University, Sally completed a major in cinema and a minor in organic chemistry. She sought work in restoration and was hired straight out of university by a small company that rescued, restored and warehoused priceless films. It was during a casual conversation with colleagues that *Blunt City After Midnight* came up and they had a good laugh remembering the commercial. The official story was that the complete film had been lost in a fire in 1965. But an office old-timer said there were rumours that the film had survived. Her colleague said some years ago he had read a little-known personal memoir written by John Alberts, grandson of Thomas Alberts, the writer and director the film. In the short memoir the author claimed the film had survived in the old wing the Blunt City Film Registry. In the memoir he made an appeal to search for the lost cult film.

Sally had been intrigued by the possibility of finding a piece of history related to Blunt City, ordered the memoir and quickly read through it. The author claimed that the original reel of *Blunt City After Midnight* had not been burned, and was located in the old wing of the Registry and subsequently lost during the reorganization in the 1980s. There was no other information, just a long rant about poor archive management, lack of cultural awareness and ignorance of the avantgarde genius of Thomas Albert. But there was one other tidbit in the memoir that caused Sally to raise her eyebrows. The author stated that the Alberts family could trace its roots back to Captain Blunt, and therefore the film has double the historical significance.

Sally came out of her daydream as felt Joseph stare. He shrugged. "Don't worry, Sally. You don't have to worry about perusing these shelves. The lost film reel won't be there." He winked as though they had been friends for centuries. "I would know, I helped catalogue all of these reels over the past few weeks." He pointed down the hall. "If *Blunt City After Midnight* is anywhere at all it will be in the back of the storeroom."

Sally followed Joseph's heavy steps down the long corridor hoping he was right. If she didn't find the lost reel in the storeroom, she knew she would attack the shelves, and that would mean days of work. That would be difficult to justify as her company had allotted her only three days to locate the reels, and depending on their conditions, they would cover restoration costs and sell it back to the Blunt City Film Registry. It was a bit of a long-shot, but everyone in the office was too curious and management was easily convinced to invest some money in the search.

Sally wrinkled her nose at the smell of vinegar that assaulted her senses as she opened the cardboard box. "Do they all smell this bad?"

"I'm not sure, I've only opened a few and there must be two hundred boxes." Joseph smiled. "So, Sally, what do you do in your time off?"

Sally cast him a sidelong glance. She wasn't sure if it was just casual talk or if he was hitting on her. She really wasn't in the mood for chit-chat. She was too excited to think she might actually find *Blunt City After Midnight*. "Not much."

"Have you ever been to the Electric Poobah?" Joseph asked.

Sally deliberately kept her eyes on the reels as she sifted through the box. "Of course."

"Ever been to the monthly 70s dance contest?"

Sally tried not to imagine the lumbering Joseph sweating on the dance floor. "Once or twice."

"They're pretty cool, huh?" Joseph grated his steel folding chair on the tiles as he slid himself closer. "I was in the last contest when Lester beat The Manakin. You can see me in the Blather video cheering Lester on when he does his trademark Pizzaz." He slid another inch closer. "Lester's a friend of mine, you know."

"Oh yeah."

"I mean, we don't hang out but we nod to each other in the disco." Sally thought Joseph spoke too loudly in the small, windowless room. "It's a man thing."

"It really doesn't sound like your close." Sally cursed herself for uttering more than two syllables, but her comments seemed to glide over him.

"I made it to the second round." Joseph grinned over her shoulder. "That means I beat out half of the dancers. But then I was eliminated."

"Mm." Sally tried to keep her back turned but Joseph shifted in his seat and leaned on the steel table.

"It's not easy, you know." He put two fingers on the table and kicked them up one at a time. It took a moment for Sally to realize that he was trying to mime dance steps. Sally could see he was trying too hard and thought she should discourage him somehow. Ten words into the conversation and she knew they had nothing in common. Joseph rambled on like a freight train. "It's easy to sign up, but it's not easy to get past the first round. Even if you know all the basic moves like the hustle, or the car wash, you really gotta feel them. You have to be able to transmit your vibes to the judges."

Sally studied a film reel. "I guess you're a good dancer."

Joseph grinned. "Yeah, I know it looks like I can't dance, but I'm pretty funky." His bloated cheeks wobbled to some unheard beat as he clicked his tongue. He stopped suddenly and flushed. Sally realized it was because she had crinkled her nose. She had just opened another box and was hit by a wave of vinegar. She couldn't figure out how to smooth over the situation and decided to hold her tongue. Joseph cleared his throat. "You know. Anyway."

"I don't see anything promising in this box." Sally swept her hand over the stack of reels. "Aside from the fact that they're in poor conditions, theses reels are too new to be from the nineteen-twenties."

Joseph nodded. "They look like they're from the fifties. Communist witch hunt time." Sally felt his stare as she opened another box. "You know that Thomas Alberts was a communist?"

Sally looked up. "What? Where did you get that information from?"

Joseph grinned over his juicy tidbit. "I read some old articles published by him in the early nineteen hundreds in a newspaper called *The Daily Proletariat*. I looked up the publication in the library. It had some pretty good readership numbers in Blunt City from the late eighteen hundreds until WWII. It shut down in the mid nineteen fifties when the Red Panic hit Cananda and United States."

Sally sat back in the hard chair. "Wow. I never would have guessed that a fairly successful director would have been a communist."

"I know, it's crazy." Joseph enthused. "To think that three hundred and fifty years later Captain Blunt's great-great something-or-other was commie."

"Well, assuming that Thomas Alberts really was a direct descendent." Sally said. "There really isn't proof of that."

Joseph started. "Well, in the memoirs his grandson John Alberts provides documents."

"It's questionable documentation and there is also a one-hundred-year span without any at all." Sally shook her head. "There is no solid proof the Alberts family was related to Captain Blunt."

"I've read it in the Blunt City Actors Archive." Joseph insisted. "It's written in his official biography for Thomas Alberts."

"I bet they didn't cite any sources," Sally countered. "There is no actual documentation provided for the entire eighteenth century. His grandson wrote down anecdotal evidence passed along by supposed relatives."

"Yeah, but those relatives were real people. I mean, I'm sure we could find their birth certificates and prove they were real." Joseph flushed and shook his head vigorously. "And why would John Alberts lie about it? And why would Thomas Alberts, who was a communist and who probably hated European conquistadors, have lied about his family tree?"

Sally thought that Joseph couldn't properly defend the claims but didn't want to argue. She had to find an orphan film, but she was genuinely curious about Alberts's past as communist writer. "The communist articles Thomas Alberts wrote didn't cause him political problems for his film making?"

Joseph nodded. "Actually, I think it did get him into hot water. Alberts wrote a bunch of articles when he started his acting career, but before he became a writer and director, he stopped writing in *The Daily Proletariat*."

"Huh. Interesting." Sally tapped her lip. "Did you read anything about or trials or Alberts getting blacklisted?"

Joseph looked a little too pleased for Sally's liking. "Nothing. But the commie investigations didn't start until the Red Panic was roaring in the mid nineteen forties. The last article Thomas Alberts wrote was twenty years earlier, just two years before he filmed *Blunt City After Midnight*."

Sally couldn't stop her questions; the unexpected news had her hooked. "What did the articles say?"

Joseph rubbed his hands and reached into his satchel. As he pulled out some photocopies Sally wondered if he had planned this in advance to impress her. Sally thought about her big, smiling picture on the company website. And her scantily clad beach photo pic on her Blather profile. She thought about taking it down when Joseph put one of the photocopies in front of her. "This one is from 1919. Alberts talks about unionising the Blunt City Actors Guild."

Sally lifted the paper and squinted at the poor-quality copy of old ink. She wished she had worn her glasses instead of her one-prescription-shy-of-seeing contact lenses. The article was a flamboyant speech calling for actors to start their own union. She looked up at Joseph. "Alberts wrote this ten years before the Blunt City Actors Guild came into being. Was he part of it?"

Joseph shook his head violently. "No! That's the crazy thing. He wrote this kinda inflammatory stuff for years, but when the Guild came together, he never joined." He gave her a smug look and rubbed his thumb against his fingers. "I guess once he began making real money he gave up on the cause."

Sally's eyes fell on the article. "Or maybe he just didn't want to risk his budding director's career."

"But, you, know. I mean, it's pretty crazy, right?" Joseph leaned until he bumped her shoulder. "To think that a major Blunt City director was a red."

Sally slid her chair to the side. "I highly doubt he was a Soviet. You know, politically speaking." Sally picked up another article. "In the first article he's writing about better pay and working hours, not about conquering countries and forcing them under a single regime."

"Yeah, but it's a slippery slope." Joseph snorted. "It's like drugs. You start with marijuana and the next thing you know you're doing crack-cocaine."

Sally frowned. "That's a ridiculous comparison to make." She watched Joseph flush. Sally knew she was too blunt, but Joseph was irritating. His come-ons were pathetically over the top but she didn't want to be cruel. Sally sighed and softened her tone. "What I meant to say is that he's talking about worker's rights, not politics. In the second article he writes about contracts." Sally tapped the photocopy. "I didn't know that actors were coerced into signing multi year contracts. Alberts writes that producers could force actors to work every day until the shooting was done."

Joseph shrugged. "It's acting, not coal mining."

"What does that matter?" Sally felt a flash of irritation. "That doesn't mean you can make a person work every day for a month straight."

"Haven't you seen actors in onset interviews?" Joseph thrust out his chin. "They're always in their trailers drinking cocktails and smoking. Then they come out, say a few stupid things and disappear back into their trailers to lounge about."

"That's not true." Sally shook her head at his bigotry. "Actors do their job just like anyone else. If anything, they probably work more hours. And the ones that aren't famous have to work other jobs to make ends meet."

"Yeah, making a killing on tips waiting in restaurants."

Sally wondered if he misread Joseph's conversation for an advance. If he was trying to come-on to her, it was the worst attempt ever. "Anyway, I've got work to do. I need to find the orphan reel." She gave him a hard stare. "And not because Thomas Alberts might be related to Captain Blunt. Not at all. I wan to find it because *Blunt City After Midnight* is a historical piece of film and should be salvaged."

Joseph gave an embarrassed shrug. "Sure, I totally agree. It's a piece of history." He loomed. "So? What do you think about Albert's articles?"

"What do you mean?" Sally opened another box.

"Well, maybe unions were a good thing a hundred years ago. But what's the point now?" Joseph grunted as he picked up a large box and put it on the table. "We're not unionized and things are fine."

Sally realized she hadn't ever really thought of unionization. For her unions were a thing of the past. Maybe useful once, but no longer today. But she just couldn't find it in her heart to agree with the greasy

Joseph. “Well, maybe with jobs like ours in the modern world everything is fine. But what about factory jobs?”

“There are no factory jobs anymore.” Joseph sounded like he was stating the Gospel truth. “Everything is made in China and mined in Africa.”

Sally looked up at Joseph. His face wasn't mocking, it was matter-of-fact. This was something else she hadn’t thought much about. Suddenly she felt ignorant. She knew virtually everything she bought was made over seas, but that’s just how things were. She had read that factory conditions in China were improving, so there was no need to feel guilty, yet somehow Joseph’s words had triggered a sense of shame. Sally had a good life. A well-paying job with regular work hours, a great group of friends and an easygoing roommate. Was her life maybe too privileged? “I don't know. But I don't think that the only reason for a union is for back-breaking work. You even said it yourself; acting isn't coal mining but Alberts fought for better pay conditions and working hours so actors wouldn't be exploited.”

Joseph drummed his fingers on the steel table. “Then Alberts gave up on it when he became a rich director.”

“Maybe.” Sally couldn’t think of a rebuttal and was upset at her growing unease. She felt a queasy feeling in her stomach. “But his ideas took hold and ten years later there was a union.”

“Yeah, I guess.” Joseph opened another box. “But maybe that's why it costs so much to make a movie.”

Sally balked. “How do you figure that?”

Joseph pulled out a putrid smelling reel. “They pay actors too much so it costs us a fortune to see a movie.”

“No way.” Sally shook her head. “There's no way that an actor's salary is the only cause of expensive films.”

“Maybe not the only cause.” Joseph opened another large box and peered inside. “But it's a big one.”

"What about the producers and studios?" Sally set down a nameless but promising reel and crossed her arms. "Don't you think they are the ones driving up the costs?"

"Maybe." Joseph shrugged. "Anyway, soon all movies will be AI generated and actors will be out of work." He sneered. "They should probably lower their salaries if they want to keep their jobs playing make-believe."

"That's not right." Sally felt a hot flash of anger pitch her forward involuntarily, then she sat back. "Why should actors reduce their pay because of artificial intelligence? And it's not make-believe, it's a form of art and expression."

"They're just pretending to be other people. And AI will take over the world of cinema no matter what." Joseph said smugly. "If they don't like it, it's not my problem. I'm tired of paying so much for two hours in a theatre."

"The high movie ticket prices are not the actors fault." Sally insisted. "And I want to see real human actors directed by real human directors in the films I watch."

"I would too, if a movie cost only five dollars, but tickets cost at least three times what they should."

Sally shook her head and looked back at the film reels. She was here to find a piece of history and not chat politics with an ogling archivist. She felt troubled by the odd sensation of guilt that Joseph had instilled in her. The unexpected turn of the conversation had her questioning many of her own beliefs about the world she lived in. Sally had come to look for a lost film reel, but the experience had been soured. She couldn't quite retrace how the conversation had started and how she finished up arguing about workers rights. Sally picked up a film reel with the smudged words *Blunt City Af—* and let it hover in front of her eyes. Instead of elation she felt another pang of guilt.

End

ENRICO PICCHI

THE MAN WHO SAID TOO MUCH

The Blunt City Chronicles

The Blunt City Chronicles Volume I:
The Man Who Said Too Much:

Chapter 1: An Odd Visitor:

In a blink he was standing in the middle of the room. Russell Dymek turned around and considered the the strange but well-known place. It looked like his bedroom, but the colours were off. The walls should have been off-white, yet they were a pale green. Not quite a sickly colour, but just odd enough to be unsettling. The furniture seemed to be all in the same place, but the cherrywood had lost its reddish hue and seemed darker. They were also of different sizes. The dresser was wider, and the night tables were shorter. The vanity seemed to have the same footprint, but he was certain it was at least a handspan taller than he remembered it. The mirror, Russell thought. The mirror wasn't right. It wasn't quite a funhouse reflection, nor was it a kaleidoscope, but his features were distorted. He felt a moment of panic as he wondered if his face was actually disfigured. There was no way for him to check, so he inspected his hands instead. He looked at his palms, then he turned them over. They seemed to look right, except for the slightly green-grey tint.

It took all of Russell's willpower not to look at the bed. It wasn't the once-familiar pink and white duvet that was now a bleeding fuchsia that troubled him. Nor was it the size of the bed. It had been a queen sized, but now he was certain it was a king. What disturbed Russell was that his own body was sleeping in it next to his wife Heather. Russell was standing at the foot of his bed, in his pressed, grey pajamas, staring at his own sleeping form. He found it disturbing, and felt compelled to reach out and touch his own shoulder, but something stopped him. The only reason why he didn't panic and cry out was that he was certain he was still alive. Both Russells. He was standing and breathing just as his sleeping form was doing the same. Just seconds before, sleeping-Russell had turned over from his wife, jammed his hand under the pillow and garbled out a snore. Now sleeping-Russell slept soundly. That part made sense.

What made no sense was that he, wide awake Russell, was walking around his almost-room in the dead of the night while his wife and sleeping-Russell were tucked into their bed. He had already pinched both arms enough times to be confident that he was real. Or at least, as real as a dozen pinch tests could prove that he was indeed himself. He was tempted to reach out and pinch sleeping-Russell, but somehow, he knew he couldn't do it. That was the other thing that made no sense to him. He felt an itching in his mind that seemed to say *'Russell, you have to wait'*. But wait for what?

With a sigh Russell, nipped his pajama legs, bent his knees and made to sit on his bed. With a start he quickly stood back up. It was that damned mind-itch again. It told him he shouldn't do that. It didn't tell him not to wake sleeping-Russell, it just seemed to tell him not to sit on the bed. The mind-itch communicated without words. It was almost like a strong suggestion. No, Russell thought. It was like a no-smoking sign. That was it. Somehow, the mind-itch showed Russell sitting on the end of his bed with a big 'X' over his own image. So, Russell stood and paced.

There was a good enough room to pace in. His bedroom was large with big, paned-glass windows. Russell widened his eyes, rushed to a window, stuck his hand between the drapes and pulled one aside. He was greeted by a large owl nestled in his oak tree, looking at him with great disapproval. Outside it was dark and hazy. Not smoggy, it was an undefined, gossamer haze. Suddenly, the mind-itch put an 'X' over Russell peering outside. He tried to resist the mind-itch and kept squinting, but slowly his hand began to release the drape. The drape was heavy and was getting heavier. Like a ton of fabric weighing on his arm it slowly pushed downwards and across the window. Finally, it settled itself, completely blocking Russell's view of the outside world. Fuzzy as it was, it was still reassuringly his world. Or so he thought. What if this was the underworld? Maybe he really was dead.

Russell rushed back to the bed and looked down upon it. It was quiet, too quiet. But after a few moments of intense staring, he saw sleeping-Russell's chest rise and fall. Heather stirred for a moment and went still, her breathing light. Russell pinched himself and winced. It seemed like he was alive. But damn it, there were two of him! Sleeping-Russell and awake-Russell. Which of the two was the real him? How could he solve this problem if that damned mind-itch wouldn't let him shake sleeping-Russell to figure it out? Between the two Russells they would have to come to some sort of conclusion.

There was a low groan and Russell snapped his head around, frantically trying to determine the source. He felt the floor vibrate as the groaning became louder. The furniture began to shake violently. His bed with sleeping-Russell and Heather became a blur of fuchsia. He wanted to flatten himself on the carpet but the damned mind-itch had beaten him to the punch and put a giant 'X' over flattened-Russell. Just as he was about to scream the groaning stopped and all was still. In the middle of the room, hovering in the air was an ethereal, greenish light.

On tiptoe, Russell stalked towards it, silent as a cat. Simultaneously he wondered two things. Did it make sense to move towards it? And if so, what was the point of tiptoeing? Russell planted his feet firmly on the shaggy rug and waited. He was tired of the whole thing. Let the light do something, say something, give him a sign! That's what dreamy lights did in the movies. They spoke with the voice of God. But other times the light spoke with the voice of a demon. Russell took a couple of steps back. Just in case.

Slowly, the hovering green light elongated. It reached up to the ceiling and down to the floor. It also became wider, or maybe it took on more depth, Russell really wasn't sure. But he was absolutely sure the light was growing brighter. A lot brighter. So much so that he had to avert his eyes. There was also a hum. Very quickly it became loud and piercing. It grew in frequency, undulating and washing through him. The light was so bright he had to shut his eyes. The hum grew to a deafening roar that forced him to clamp his hands over his ears. He gritted his teeth to stifle a scream but it was impossible. He bellowed into the roaring hum as the bright light enveloped him completely. Then it all stopped. Slowly Russell uncovered his ears and opened his eyes.

"Oh my God!" Russell covered his eyes again. "God no! Wh-what? What are you?" He stared through his fingers and shut his eyes again. "Please! Please don't hurt me!"

A low, juddering voice spoke. "Human, we mean you no harm."

Russell looked through his fingers. "Are you sure?" It didn't seem like the smartest thing to say, but Russell was a prudent man. Better safe than sorry.

The wavering voice spoke again. "Human, we mean you no harm."

Slowly, Russell pulled his hands from his face. It was surprisingly difficult. He pried his eyes open. That was even more difficult. He tried not to gape because he knew it was rude. But he just couldn't help it, his jaw hung wide open. Standing before him was a long, bean of a creature that had pale green skin, huge eyes, a small mouth with virtually no nose and a cone head. It wore a loose, forest-green cloak with the hood pulled back. Russell thought it must have been more than seven feet tall with, long slim limbs, hands and bare feet. For Russell, that was the icing on the cake. Who walked around in the dead of the night without shoes? Russell swallowed hard. "Who are you? Where did you come from? What do you want?"

"Human," it said. "We have come to lift your restraints."

"My restraints?" Russell looked at his limbs. They were unfettered. What did the green bean mean by that? "Who are you? Where did you come from?"

The being stood perfectly still, only its fish lips droned out its wobbly voice. "Human, we come from a parallel universe."

Russell nodded. He was making progress, even if the green bean was clearly insane. Slow but steady wins the race, the thought. Russell took a deep breath. "Which universe?" He felt it was a logical question.

The green bean was unmoving. "Human, you wouldn't understand."

Russell nodded again. The green bean was probably right. But still, this was his house and he didn't like the idea of being liquidated so quickly by an intruder. "Are you responsible for the two 'me's? You know, this 'me' and the sleeping one?"

"Yes," the green bean said. "We have that immense power."

Russell stroked his chin. "Would you care to elaborate?"

"Human, you also are from a parallel universe," the green bean pointed at Russell and then to sleeping-Russell. "We are using this you to reach that other you."

Russell nodded dumbly. He was certain the dimensional green bean could be considered clinically insane. His quick diagnosis would also explain about fifty percent of the home invasion. But what about the other, and clearly more significant, fifty percent? Russell cleared his throat. "I'm really not sure I follow."

"Human, you are you but not that you," the green bean pointed to the bed, then back at him. "You are this you that we will use to reach that other you which is still you even though it is not you."

Russell knew he was in way over his head. "Ok, I'm both 'me's. Sure. I was able to figure that out myself. But how? And why?"

"Human, you are not listening. Or more likely, you are not understanding." The green bean gave him a patronizing look. "You are this you, not that you."

If this had been his daughter Michelle's fiancé Greg speaking, Russell would have accused him of being a crackhead. "I'm two different 'me's. But still me?"

"Human, you are this you which is from a parallel universe. You are not that you which resides in this universe."

Russell hated these debates. And this one was far worse than when Heather would force him to watch Blather documentaries on quantum physics and alternate realities and then make him talk about the nonsense after. "Fine. Let's say I'm from another dimension. Universe. Whatever." Russell pointed to sleeping-Russell. "What about him?"

"Human, we just explained this to this you. That you is from this universe," it said. "This you is from a parallel universe."

Russell raised his eyebrows. "How many other universes are there?"

"Many."

Russell frowned. For a creature that claimed to be powerful and able to use interdimensional space, it was surprisingly imprecise. Russell had studied accounting and was a successful sales director. He really needed hard figures to make his clock tick. "Can't you put a number to it?"

"We could, but there would be too many zeros behind that number for your feeble mind to comprehend."

Russell put his hands on his hips. "Try me."

"Nine. With this many zeros." The green bean waved a hand in the air and Russell gaped. An indescribable number of sparkling zeros paraded before his eyes. Lines and lines upon lines of zeros. Then the entire room filled with zeros. They pushed at him and threatened to blow out his expensive, recently restored pane-glass windows. Or sleeping-Russell's windows. He really couldn't be sure who would have to foot the bill.

Russell looked desperately for a dollar sign before the number nine that led the zero-parade. He whispered feverishly to himself. "If I had a ten percent cut of those universes, I would own this world."

"Human, it is time."

"Time for what?"

"Time for the restraints to be lifted." The green been said. "We will act."

"Are you using the royal we, or is there someone with you?"

"We are single and we are all." The green bean said. "Human, prepare yourself."

"For what?" Russell was irritated. "How can a man prepare if he doesn't know what he's preparing for?" It was basic business logic, he thought. Know the plan. Know the variables. Take decisive action.

The long green bean shook its head. Russell thought sadly. Or was it a head shake of disdain? The green bean warbled. "Human, your mind cannot comprehend."

Russell had to agree. He couldn't understand a damned thing that the green bean was saying. Perhaps a more colloquial approach would make the difference. "What's your name?"

"Human, you may call us Gizmo."

"Gizmo doesn't really sound like an alien name." Thanks to Heather, Russell had seen at least one hundred alien movies, so he had a pretty good feel for extra-terrestrials. "I would have thought it would have been more guttural. Or maybe a series of pops and clicks."

"Human, you could never pronounce our true name." Gizmo gave him a knowing look. Finally, Russell thought. The green bean seemed to show some kind of empathy.

"Ok, I'm not going to press the point." Russell sighed. "But could you stop calling me 'human'? My name is Russell."

Gizmo raised a long arm. "Russell-human, heed our words! We will lift your restraints!" The green bean shook. Or perhaps it was Russell's room turning upside down. This out of body alien dimensional dream experience was getting creepy. He heard the green bean call out to him. "Russell-human, we're over here."

Russell realized he was facing the closet. "Sorry, I lost my bearings." He shook his head. "Why do you want to lift my restraints?"

"Because we can."

Russell put his hands to his hips. "You know, if I answered one of my clients that way I would lose a sale."

"We want nothing from you."

"I have to disagree with that statement."

Gizmo seemed to ponder. Or so Russell hoped. This time the green bean didn't make any facial gestures. Russell was good at reading faces, but this damned alien was impossible to figure out. "Russell-human, you may have a point."

"Finally!"

"But we don't care."

"No, no, that's not right. Let me explain something to you." Russell cupped his hands and moved them back and forth between him and the green bean. "It's all about give and take, you know. It's the basis of the client salesman relationship. You need to sympathize with me if you want to make the sale. Gizmo, we need to find common ground."

Gizmo began to glow and the room began to shake "Russell-human, heed our words! Your restraints will be lifted! You will begin a new species of ultra-unrestrained Russel-superhumans!"

"I really didn't understand anything that you just said."

"Sleep, Russell-human. Sleep."

Chapter 2: Breakfast Reality:

"Hon? The alarm has gone off three times." Russell felt a hand gently shake him. "Are you ok?"

With a sigh Russell opened his eyes. He was face down in the bed, his face buried in a fluffy pillow. He stirred, stretched and rolled over on his back. Russell blinked and squinted. "Morning."

Heather leaned down to give him a kiss. "Morning, sleepy head." She gave him a cockeyed glance and put a hand to his forehead. "You don't feel feverish."

Russell continued his stretch. "I'm a little tired, but I feel ok."

Heather slid off the bed. "Ok. Come on downstairs. Breakfast is on the table."

Russell raised his head and let it fall into the cushion. He rubbed his cheek, the rough stubble scratching his palm. There was something in the back of his mind but he couldn't quite focus on it. It was as though there was a little voice calling out to him, trying to tell him something. He tried to focus on it but it eluded him. It felt like a tiny inner doppelganger was furiously waving his arms and shouting, but he couldn't hear the words.

With a noisy grunt he pushed himself up and smacked his lips. He patted his paunch and rubbed his bald head. Russell started losing his hair was he was twenty, by thirty he had decided to trim it to zero. It became his every other day ritual with an electric trimmer and he was thankful to have a fairly round head with generally soft features and an easy smile. In a suit and tie he needed to look like a salesman and not like some video game psycho assassin.

With considerable effort Russell swung his legs down to the ground and winced as he pushed himself upwards. He really would have to take time to exercise and start rehabilitation as Rebecca, his youngest daughter, had been nagging him to do. He had put on twenty pounds in two years since he stopped playing tennis. Now his knee was really starting to be a problem with the extra weight. He walked over to the vanity to have a look at the bags he was certain would be hanging under his eyes.

The moment he saw his reflection he felt a rush and gasped. Suddenly, the dream came back to him. The strange colours, the sounds, the noise, the tall, green alien. A tall, green alien! Barefoot in his bedroom! And it wanted to do something to him! An experiment of some sort, but from another dimension! No, that wasn't it. Now he remembered. The alien was from another dimension. Or was it a universe? And what did it want? To un-restrain him. He frowned. What could that possibly mean?

Russell looked around to locate his slippers and strangely found them in front of the closet instead of by the bed. He padded across the thick carpet and slipped them on. He walked to the door, took his housecoat off the hook and slipped on his shoulders. He wrapped the belt and tugged it tight and grimaced at his paunch. He never had been a slim man, but this new bulge was putting his suits under duress.

With a hand on the banister, Russel winced his way down with every step. There was no doubt his knee was getting worse. Regular walking wasn't a problem, but stairs were getting to be a nuisance. It was another excuse not to put into action his New Year's resolution for taking the stairs up to his office at work. He gratefully landed on the foyer floor, turned left and walked into the kitchen. Heather was busy at the stove making coffee while his cereal and milk was waiting for him at the breakfast table.

"Hezzy, I had a really weird dream last night."

Heather looked up. "Oh yeah? About what?"

"You'll think I'm crazy."

Heather laughed. "I have crazy dreams all the time." She frowned. "I tell you about them but you never listen."

Russell shrugged. "Yeah. Sorry."

Heather walked to the kitchen table with two mugs of coffee. "So, tell me your crazy dream."

Russell tried to gather his thoughts as he spooned cereal into his mouth. He hardly ever remembered his dreams, and even when he did, they normally escaped his mind by breakfast. "It was like an out of body experience."

Heather cocked an eyebrow and leaned forward. "Really? This sounds interesting."

"Yeah, I guess." Russell suddenly felt like an idiot, but there was not turning back now. Not when Heather's interest was piqued. "There was an alien from another dimension. Or maybe he said universe."

Heather's eyes widened and she grinned. "You're kidding me! What did the alien look like?" She always got excited about aliens. "Was it a grey, or a reptilian?"

Russell shook his head. "Neither. I mean, it was green with an elongated head, but it wasn't either of those two."

Heather pursed her lips. "Maybe it was a hybrid?"

Russell frowned. "They can mate?"

"Of course not!" Heather winked. "The hybrid would be made via genetic engineering!"

Russell grimaced. "Yeah. Maybe. I really don't know. Let's just forget about it."

"Come on," Heather leaned her head on his shoulder. "I'm just teasing. Go on, I'm really interested."

"Well, I was in our bedroom watching us sleep." Russell felt even stupider when Heather widened her eyes. He stared into her two hazel orbs. "Then the room began shaking and there was a flash of light. Now it gets really stupid."

"Go on, Russ." She grinned. "You know I love this stuff."

That was the problem, Russell thought. He gave his wife an embarrassed smile. "Then this super-tall, thin green alien wearing a cloak appeared in the middle of our bedroom." It sounded ridiculous coming out of his mouth but Heather was eating it up.

"Wow! So, no spaceship?" She made a sphere-like gesture with her hands and then expanded them like an explosion. "The alien just materialized out of a flash of light?"

"Yeah." Russell spooned in another mouthful of cereal, chewed and swallowed. "And the weirdest part was that he was barefoot."

Heather frowned, then nodded. "I would hope so. You know shoes are not allowed in the bedroom."

Russell nodded. That was true, but how would the alien have known? "So, then he began talking. There was just one alien, but he kept saying 'we' this and 'we' that."

"You mean like the royal we?"

Russell spoke through a mouthful. "That's what I asked him."

"What did he say?"

"I actually can't remember." Russell searched his mind. Maybe the green bean hadn't answered him. He looked at Heather and felt his ears burn. "The alien said his name was Gizmo."

Heather gave a hearty laugh. "What? No way! The alien said his name was Gizmo?" She giggled. "That doesn't sound like an alien name."

"I know." Russell spooned into his mouth the last of his cereal. "I told him so."

Her whole face lit up. "And what did he say to that?"

"I can't remember that bit either." Russell thought hard but it didn't come to him. Still, he was amazed so much of the dream remained so vivid in his mind.

"So?" Heather pushed on his arm. "What did Gizmo want with you?"

"Oh, right! That was actually the weirdest part." Russell crossed his wrists. "He said he would lift my restraints."

Heather put a hand to her mouth. "You were tied down?"

"No," Russell gulped his coffee and shook his head. "That's what's weird. I was standing up in my pajamas. My hands were free"

Heather furrowed her brow. "So, what do you think he meant?"

Russell shrugged. "I don't know."

"Is that it?"

"I'm afraid so."

Heather nodded, smoothed back her long blond hair and smiled. "Well, I still think it's a pretty cool dream." She cleared away his bowl. "You should write it down. You know I keep a diary of my dreams."

"Yeah, I know." Russell gulped his coffee.

"So will you write it down?" She looked at him and scrunched her nose. "Gotcha. I'll write it down in my diary. Like I said, it's a cool dream, we shouldn't lose it."

Russell nodded. What did she do with diaries upon diaries of dreams anyway? "Well thanks."

Heather loaded the dishwasher. "Remember, you have to pick up Becca at the train station after work. She's going to be in town over the weekend."

"Right, I'll pick her up."

"Blunt City Central. She comes in at 5:15pm." Heather gave him the eye. "Don't forget and don't be late."

Chapter 3: Lifting the Restraints:

Russell's maneuvered his large, company sedan deftly into his designated parking place at Rave2Engrave. He opened the door and slid out of the seat and winced as his foot hit the ground. He shut the car door and grimaced at the large, pink and blue company sign. For decades, it had been *Rave Engraving*, written in sober black letters on a white background. Then Peter died six months ago and his cokehead twenty-two-year-old son decided to, as he put it, 're-freshen' the company logo and changed the name. The madness had cost the company a fortune in signs, plaques, pens, notepads, and gadgets of all kinds. Not to mention embarrassment at the juvenile social network name.

With a wince and a limp Russell walked past the empty car space with a gigantic brass plaque that read *'Dynamo Rave Esq, CEO & Visionary'.* The buffoon had the plaque on his corner office door sized up five times and hoisted on a pole in parking so as to bring shame upon them all each time they walked by it. The loose cannon was the son of late CEO Peter and the grandson of the founder, Walter Rave. Peter had been a good man and had tragically dropped dead in the office last year to the shock of the company. Walter, who had already been retired before his son's death but would occasionally come to the office, had never been seen since. Russell also suspected that Walter had little love for his druggie grandson.

The twenty-two-year-old Dynamo was becoming a serious problem for the company. Russell hoped that he would sit in his father's mansion sniffing cocaine and draining the family bank account only to wait for Rave2Engrave to fill it back up. But no, the schizoid was determined to roll into work at the crack of noon, just in time to ruin lunch for him and the other directors. He had hired his own gadget marketing manager who conflicted with Cathy's own skilled team. Cathy had been brilliant over the last decade devising strategies which helped Russell generate new sales opportunities. Dynamo was putting all of her work at risk.

Russell felt his leg unstiffen as he entered the late nineteenth century building on the harbor front of Blunt Lake, just outside of the downtown core. He said good morning to the receptionist, eyed the stairs and veered for the elevator that Walter had installed in the archaic building. Walter had established his corrugated embossing rolls workshop here in 1963, when most of the block was rundown and cheap real-estate. The man had never even finished high school but he had a knack for business and machining. With a few used lathes and a questionable milling machine he began his journey making parts and engraved rollers.

His son Peter had Walter's passion for technology and graduated as a mechanical engineer. Peter had been a great technical mind and agreed with Russell that expansion was necessary for the business to thrive. The two had thought up conveyors to move the finished cardboard boxes and Peter had worked with the engineering manager Mark to design the prototype. Peter trusted Russell to sell the simple machine to a small local company after Russell had convinced him it was necessary to squeeze their way into a larger market. Their first idea hadn't even had a working prototype when Russell managed the first sale. The plan had worked, and Peter asked Russell to leave his position as accounting manager to take the post of Sales Director. Russell had accepted fifteen years ago and the company grew from fifty employees to more than one hundred today.

The elevator opened on the third floor where Russell's office was located along with the board of directors. Cathy Hughes, Marketing and Accounts Manager, Mark Ciobanu, Engineering Manager, John Wang, Production Manger, and Charlotte Flores, Finance and Accounting Manager. Then there was Dynamo's massive corner office. The drughead had enlarged Peter's old office, knocking the wall down of the neighbouring meeting room to create a massive cavern so his creative juices would flow better. Apparently, Peter's four hundred square foot office had stifled the poor boy.

Russell looked at the small plaque on his oak office door with pride. '*Russell Dymek, Sales Director*'. He looked left and frowned. '*Dynamo Rave Esq, CEO & Visionary*'. Did the junkie even know what the title esquire meant? Russell knew that Dynamo hadn't the vaguest clue what 'visionary' meant. Shortly after his father's death last year Dynamo had abandoned his studies in mechanical engineering at Blunt University to conquer the corner office. Russell couldn't understand why. At Dynamo's rate of study, and with the right bribes, he might have completed his degree in about five more years, giving him plenty of time to snort coke. It would have been perfect as Dynamo would have joined the company long after Russell, Mark and Cathy had retired. But no, the junkie had invaded the building and was now their problem. If Russell hadn't been worried about keeping the balance in the office he would have told Dynamo to take a hike.

The door shut with a soft click and Russell tossed his briefcase on a chair. He took off his coat and hung it on the hanger, then he walked to his desk. He sat with a wince, flipped open his laptop and turned it on. He skimmed through his agenda and licked his lips. It could be a very promising morning. Boxen Industries was a client he had won over a decade ago and they had since purchased several rollers and two small conveyor systems. Russell was trying to close a deal for a large, modular conveyor system that would shuttle their boxes from the production floor, up into the air, over the raw material warehouse and loading bay and down to the finished product warehouse on the other side. It was an ambitious and challenging project and he had called both Mark and Cathy into the meeting that he had scheduled at 10:00am. It was perfectly scheduled. At that time, the druggie would still be sleeping off a bender.

There was a sharp knock on the door and Mark walked in. "Morning Russ."

"Morning Mark." Russell said. "The technical drawings are ready?"

"Yeah, Cathy is putting the finishing touches on them." Mark sunk into the seat and grinned. "This could be a big one for us."

Russell nodded. "It will be, Mark. There is that pain in the neck of Hector Wallace, but I can handle him."

Mark laughed and shook his head. "I have no idea how you handle Wallace. The man's a total asshole."

Russell shrugged. "It comes with the job. I'd like to tell him to take a hike but we can't afford to lose this sale." He leaned on his desk. "If we get this kit installed and spread the word we've got a good chance with the big multinationals."

"Yeah, this could be huge." Mark agreed. "If you give the news of the Boxen sale on your trip to Germany you'll have the big players paying attention to us."

There was a soft knock on the door and Mark and Russell called out in unison. Cathy opened the door carefully, stepped inside and smiled. "Good morning, Russ. The documents are ready and so is the speaking order for the presentation." She gave Russell an embarrassed look. "Sorry, but I have to do the new spiel."

Russell groaned and put his head in his hands. "But the junkie isn't even going to be part of the meeting."

"Russell!" Cathy sat down next to Mark. "Don't even joke about that! What if Dynamo heard you?"

"I really don't think Dynamo has my office bugged." Russell chuckled. "He's a cokehead, not a paranoid schizophrenic."

Cathy pursed her lips. "He is not a cokehead."

Russell cocked an eyebrow. "Oh, no?"

"He's an occasional user of recreational drugs." Cathy frowned. "Not that I'm condoning it, I just want to state it for the record."

Russell gave her a sidelong glance. "You're just dotting the 'i's and crossing the 't's so to speak."

Cathy scowled. "Well, Dynamo certainly isn't Peter but he is our CEO and the last thing we need is conflict with him." She sighed. "Anyway, I have to read out the new company Mission and Vision Statement, so no laughing."

"I won't laugh." Russell clutched his stomach. "If I hear it again, I think I'll throw up my cereal."

"Russell, I'm serious." Cathy shook the heavy folder in her hands. "I need you to be smiling and professionally silent when I read this." She frowned at the two men. "I don't want to see you exchanging goofy looks with Mark."

"Yeah, alright." Russell offered her one of his sarcastic grins. "I'll take a seasickness pill before you read Dynamo's holy scripture."

Mark laughed and Cathy deepened her frown. "Russell Dymek, I am counting on you."

Russell held up two fingers. "I promise, Cath. Ok?"

Cathy looked at Russell's poker face and Mark's wide grin. "I'm counting on the both of you to behave. This is too big to mess up." Cathy blew out an exasperated sigh, stood and adjusted her jacked. She walked briskly to the door and turned to give them a determined stare. "I'll see you both in about a half hour."

Russell waited for Cathy to close the office door before he rolled out a heavy laugh with Mark. "Shit, Mark, can you believe it? We have to read the megalomaniac's Mission Statement at another meeting." He shook his head. "It really *is* becoming scripture and Cathy's our pastor."

Mark chuckled. "Give her a break, Russ. You should be thanking her. If she didn't read it you would have to."

Russell grinned. "You're right. If I had to read Dynamo's bullshit out loud, I'd puke." He shook his head. "I'll pick up a box of chocolates for Cathy tomorrow."

Mark pointed at Russell and grinned. "Smart man." He stood and straightened his tie. "I'm going to set up the projector. I'll see you in a bit."

***

During the reading of the company's Mission Statement, Russell had to clutch his knee until he winced to keep from laughing. He dared not turn to look at Mark otherwise it would have been game over. Russell really did pity Cathy. Reading Dynamo's Mission Statement took the fortitude of a meditative guru. If that wasn't enough, she also had to endure Dynamo's disastrous new marketing campaign. The junkie had weaseled in on Cathy's marketing territory insisting on numerous damaging changes, like the new company declaration. Russell tried as hard as he could to ignore the bewildered stares of the Boxen Industries representatives as Cathy read the Mission Statement out loud. Even the perpetually dour Wallace seemed confused.

Dynamo's Mission Statement could have been a stroke of brilliance, had it been used in theatre. The six hundred forty-nine-word document was so outrageously false in its scope that Russell doubted that even the most skilled dramaturgist could have possibly written a better farce. The Mission Statement began loftily, claiming that Rave2Engrave strove to surpass the most vivid dreams of its clients. Then it rapidly changed gears to state that the company was in the frontlines battling climate change and nuclear war. Following these preposterous affirmations were three paragraphs extolling the virtues of the Rave family. Then the statement dipped its toes into the murky waters of company values, declaring that it prided itself on 'boldness over honesty' and how it valued 'cunning before transparency'. It finished with the ludicrous claim that the Rave2Engrave engineering team was designing a rocket ship to 'outwit' foreign powers planning on colonizing Mars.

Every time Cathy read Dynamo's Mission Statement Russell believed she deserved a bonus. And a big one at that. How she kept a straight face was beyond his comprehension. Russell wavered between laughter and nausea at every reading. He kept his eyes glued on Cathy.

He knew he wasn't out of the woods yet. She was still reading the part about the space race so he needed to focus. Until she finished and turned the presentation over to him, he dared not look at Mark.

Finally, Cathy set down the two-page Mission Statement and smiled. She turned her head to look at the people in the room. With the stoicism of a marble statue, she ignored the baffled stares of the Boxen Industries delegation and invited Russell to present the offer for the extended conveyor system. She handed him the remote for the projector and Russell drew his hand down his face to wipe away any trace of a sarcastic grin. He bit his lip, then cleared his throat to welcome Boxen Industries and began with his presentation.

Russell was in his element in front of a crowd. He was a far cry from the stereotypical, timid accountant. He liked balancing numbers, but his real talent was in sales. The relationship with clients, being able to push Mark and his engineering team, working with Cathy to look for new markets and develop new strategies was the current that charged his batteries. The only real challenge he felt he had today was the vast scope of the project. Rave2Engrave was not really a conveyor company. Even though they had fifteen years experience, most of their sales still came from engraved rollers and small kits for embossing machines. Russell wanted to turn the business ito a fifty-fifty model to boost sales and this would be their biggest ever project.

With Mark's technical support Russell answered their questions and presented the offer. He had a long debate with Hector Wallace who questioned him on different aspects of the project. After a few minutes he realized Wallce was out of challenges, but he didn't want to upset the old man by making it seem like he had lost an arguemnt. Russell made a few concessions that caused Cathy to frown and Mark's eyes to flicker, but he kept his eyes on the prize. Russell focused his gaze of Wallace and dared to smile. The sourpuss didn't return the smile but he seemed pleased. Russell terminated the meeting with a quick joke and was rewarded with chuckles from the room. He could see the dollar signs.

Outside in the lobby Russell smiled and shook the client's hands one by one. It had been a success. He was certain the order was theirs. "Yeah, great, thanks! No, thank you! Great to see you again! Yes indeed! Sounds great! Absolutely! Wallace, you cantankerous old bastard, go fuck yourself! I'll get you the updated offer! Keep in touch! We'll talk soon! Bye!" Russell waved, turned away and walked back to his office. He opened the door, stepped inside and breathed in deeply. He congratulated himself as he shut the door behind him. He was a certain it had been a highly successful meeting. Mark and Cathy would probably balk at his freebies, but if the sale came through there was still plenty of meat on the bones. Sure, Wallace would be a thorn in his side during the duration of the project, but he could handle him. He had been dealing with the old man for years.

Russell began to whistle and had just readied himself to draft up the meeting notes when Mark burst into the room. "Russ, are you insane?"

Russell fumbled his fountain pen. "What? What's the problem?"

Mark stormed over to his desk, his hands flailing. "How could you say that?"

Russell looked at his colleague stupidly. "Mark, I think it went really well. I'm sure we'll get the sale. Maybe your engineering team will be unhappy about the extra project work but—"

"No!" Mark whispered harshly and ran to squeak close the Venetian blinds. "I know the meeting went well. You were great." Mark glared. "Right up until the end."

Russell tapped his pen on his notepad. "Do you think I gave up too easily on the redesign? It's only an extra motor and drive train on the conveyor belt. Sure, there's the servo drive and programing, but it won't cost that much. I needed to have Wallace think he won the discussion."

Mark stared at Russell and wiped his face. "Russ, you told Wallace to go fuck himself."

Russell blinked several times, then he broke out into a grin. "You clown! You almost had me there!"

"No, Russ!" Mark sat down and grabbed Russell's jacket sleeve. "I am not kidding you." He pointed behind himself. "If you don't believe me, ask Cathy! She was right there with us!"

Russell nodded. "Yeah, she was right there."

"Exactly." Mark tugged wildly at his jacked and crossed his arms.

Russell shook his head. "Mark, don't take this the wrong way, but I don't believe you." He sighed. "And I'm not in the mood for jokes. Quite frankly, I think I did a good job, all things considered. Listen, if you're unhappy with my proposal to the client, then let's talk to—hey! Where are you going?"

"To get Cathy!" Mark snapped.

The door slammed shut and Russell jolted upright. What kind of a joke was this? Mark was the engineering manager, he hardly ever joked. When he did, it was always about gears and shafts. Russell shook his head. It was all too strange. He thought hard about the end of the meeting. What had he said that could have been so offensive? He had said his goodbyes, shook hands and said he would send through the updated offer. What was the problem?

The door flew open to a red-faced Mark and a frazzled Cathy. Mark pushed Cathy forward. "Go on! Tell him!"

Cathy walked awkwardly on her heels, her hands shaking in front of her. "Russell! How could you?"

Russell pulled his face back. "How could I what?"

"Russell, you told Hector Wallace off!" Cathy's voice trembled. "You shook his hand and told him off! Then you just walked away!"

Russell turned his head and looked down. He turned back to Cathy. "This, this, what? No."

"Russell, I was out there with Boxen Industries trying to smooth things over! I was so shocked I was certain I hadn't heard right." Russell thought Cathy looked generally distraught. "The look on their faces! Oh Russell, how could you?"

Russell put his head in his hands and tried to weigh their words. These were two trusted colleagues. They had worked together for years. They were straight shooters, not pranksters. Mark and Cathy were his right and left arms. Since the death of Peter Rave, and the daily appearances of Dynamo, Russell had worked more closely than ever with the two managers. Mark and Cathy were his anchor points and helped keep Rave2Engrave on the straight and narrow. They wouldn't lie to him. "Listen, I don't know what to say. I swear, I don't remember saying that. I don't even know why I would have said it." Russell shook his heads. "There was no reason to. I had Wallace, hook, line and sinker."

Cathy sat down and took his hand. "Maybe you're just stressed. We know you're doing the work of the CEO in place of Dynamo. Plus, you have all of your own responsibilities."

Mark sat in the chair next to her. "Yeah, Cathy's right. You probably just had to let off some steam and it came out like a nervous tick."

Cathy nodded. "That's all it was, I'm sure." She continued to pet his hand. A little too frantically for Russell's liking. "I think I managed to straighten things out with Hector Wallace."

Russell looked at them and rubbed his free hand down his face. He offered a wan smile. "I don't know what to say. I'm sorry."

Cathy let go of his hand and waved. "It's fine, Russell. It was an unfortunate incident. Let's just forget about it and update the offer." She took a page that was under his hands. "I'll take care of this report with Denise, ok?"

"Yes, Ok. Thanks."

Mark stood. "Cathy's right. Let's just drop this and get back to work."

The two trailed out and closed the door. Russell sat, dumbfounded. He had no memory of telling the Hector Wallace, owner of Boxen

Industries, to take a hike. He leaned back in the chair, tense and sweating. The meeting had been almost easy. Wallace had barely challenged him at all, and once he knew he was going to get an extra motor, drive and software free of charge, he all but said yes. Wallace wouldn't have said yes to his face, he would have his purchasing manager handle it, but Russell had left the meeting certain it was in the bag. There had been no reason for him to get angry, and he hadn't felt stressed out at all.

The door swung upon to reveal a slender, seedy looking young man in a suit that looked like it had been stolen from a mafia film set. He wore an expensive gold watch, and a garish tie that clashed wonderfully with his alligator shoes. He slicked back his dark manga-like hair with his hand and widened his face into a condescending smile to display perfectly straight, white teeth. "Russ, my man! How did the meeting go with Boxen Industries?"

If ever there was a moment where Russell couldn't stomach the buffoon, it was now. "Fine, Dynamo."

"Good stuff, my man!" Dynamo jumped over the chair back to land on the seat, slamming his foot into the top of Russell's desk. "Ow, fuck! Fuck, that hurt!" He scowled at Russell as he rubbed his ankle. "Shit, Russ, you've gotta do something about that."

Russell raised an eyebrow. "I have to do something about what?"

"You know," Dynamo pointed at the desk. "That."

"Sure." Russell kept his voice even. "I'll call building maintenance and have them carve out a shoe hole."

Dynamo seemed to ponder the comment. Russell knew he was trying to figure out if he had been sarcastic. Judging by the narrowing of his eyes the junkie had succeeded in understanding. "Right." Dynamo hissed. "So, anyway. Did you get the sale?"

"They're considering our offer. It looks promising."

Dynamo threaded his fingers behind his head. "Did you give them a discount?"

Russell's eye twitched. "I offered them a free upgrade."

The chair creaked as Dynamo rocked back and forth. "Are they gonna buy my prototype?"

"The company prototype designed by Mark's team." Russell replied. Dynamo would charge into Mark's office, suggest a few wild ideas and then claim his vision had willed a drawing into reality. "I don't know yet, I have to follow up with them."

Dynamo nodded. "Can't you do that now?"

"They left half an hour ago."

With a sigh, Dynamo slouched and crossed his arms. "Why'd you schedule a meeting so early, anyway?"

"Dynamo, the meeting started at 10:00 am." Russell rubbed his forehead. This was not the right day to be putting up with the twitchy cokehead. "Office hours are 9:00 to 5:00."

"Yeah. But the office start time seems a little extreme." Dynamo pinched his lips. "Maybe I can shift that back a little."

"And what would you do about quitting time?" Russell asked.

Strangely, or perhaps not so strangely, the question genuinely seemed to stump Dynamo. "I'm not sure." He shrugged. "I can figure that out later."

Russell gritted his teeth. "You can't change business hours without causing a tsunami of problems for more than one hundred people."

For a few moments Dynamo was silent. Russell doubted the cokehead was truly considering changing office hours, but there was no way to be certain. He would have to inform Cathy, just in case. Dynamo suddenly smiled. "Did Cathy read my Mission Statement."

"She did. But Dynamo, it really needs to be pared down?"

He moved his hands in an oblong shape. "Pear?"

Russell closed his eyes and breathed out sharply through his nose. "I mean, it needs to be a lot shorter."

The first time Russell met Dynamo he was sixteen years old. He instantly recognized the spoiled brat would be trouble. Russell remembered after their informal meeting it was the only time Peter spoke openly about his son. He told Russell how much he had regretted marrying a showgirl on a whim. Peter told him she had been witty and beautiful and they had jumped into a relationship and marriage in a matter of months. She was pregnant before they married, Peter admitted that was part of it, but he thought it would work. He soon found how different they were, and the ridiculous name he consented to for his son was only one of the many examples. Two years later came the costly divorce. Peter blamed himself for Dynamo's behaviour because of the years he hadn't been part of his life. So, Peter let Dynamo run roughshod all over him. The kid needed discipline but instead he got lollipops and sports cars. It was too late to fix the problem now.

"Well, I think the Mission Statement is just the right length." Dynamo pumped his fist. "It puts our great passion into words."

"Listen, I'm busy. I think you should be too." Russell would not let the brat run roughshod over him. "Why don't you go to your office and check your emails."

Russell thought he caught a flash of anger in Dynamo's eyes. Russell didn't budge. Experience was on his side. After a few moments Dynamo smiled with angry eyes. "I think I'll go check my emails."

Russell forced out a half smile. "Have a good day, Dynamo."

Chapter 4: Confession:

The traffic around Blunt City train station in the downtown was like a beard of bees. The cars clung to every square inch of asphalt and changing lanes meant risking scratching up his bumper. Even though Russell had left work early he still managed to arrive fifteen minutes after the train pulled in. He squeezed his luxury sedan between a couple of taxis and managed to tag behind a compact car that wound through the throngs of commuters. Russell parked in a tow away zone, jumped out of the car and waved down his youngest daughter.

"Hey Becca! Over here!" Russell watched Becca turn and smile as she rolled her travel bags towards him.

"Hey dad!" Becca skidder her suitcases to a halt as Russell opened the trunk. She stood on her tiptoes for a kiss as Russell hurled her oversized bags into the back of his car. He smiled guiltily at the scowling policeman who waved him on his way.

Russell tossed his keys in the chip box, pressed the button and his car hummed to life. "Sorry I'm late, pumpkin. Traffic was terrible."

Becca smiled. "No worries, I appreciate the pickup. Taking the subway and then the bus with my bags would have been killer.

Russell eased his oversized sedan into the unending column of wheeled freedom. "What brings you home from Eastern University?"

"I don't have classes until final exams and Katie organized a disco night on the Blather Dance App." Becca gave him the same impish grin Heather used. "Like a hundred of us responded."

"Oh yeah." Russell searched his memory and came up empty. "Who's Katie?"

"Come on, dad." Becca frowned. "Michelle's friend from Blunt University." Becca snapped her fingers and bobbed her head. "You remember. The one that likes to organize cosplay dance groups."

"Oh. Sure."

"Anyway," Becca rolled her eyes. "There's a 70s dance competition at the Electric Poobah so we're having a bit of a reunion. I guess I'm filling in for Michelle."

"Oh, ok." Russell raised an eyebrow. "You're into 70s music?"

Becca grinned. "Crazy, huh? The music is as old as you are!"

"Watch it, kid!" Russell returned the grin of his youngest daughter. He didn't think he looked too bad for a fifty-five-year-old man. He could hardly believe he was only two years from early retirement. After Peter's sudden death, Heather and Russell had decided that there was more to life than the office. Heather had been working parttime in the Captain Blunt Museum for just about her entire career, from shortly after the birth of Michelle until today. Now that the girls were grown, with Michelle living out West and Becca set to graduate this year, Heather and Russell had studied their finances. He had to admit, by the standards of the average person they were rich. It didn't take much organization and investment shifting for them to plan an early out. They still hadn't told anyone except for Rebecca and Michelle who were enthusiastic about the idea. Russell grimaced at the thought of telling Mark and Cathy that he would be out the door before they were despite the fact he was the youngest of the three.

Becca poked his paunch. "Have you been going on your daily walk?"

"Absolutely." He gave her a sidelong glance. "To and from the couch."

"Dad!" Becca treated him to another eye roll. "Your knee isn't going to get any better if you don't lose the extra weight."

This was the problem with a daughter majoring in kinesiology. He got nagging treatments for free. "I've just been busy. Without Peter it's been rough."

Becca ran her hand through her long blond hair. Russell glanced at and caught her hazel eyes staring at him with intently. "No luck with Dynamo?"

Russell grimaced. "So far he hasn't overdosed."

"Dad!" Becca slapped him on the arm. "Be nice."

Every time Dynamo came up with Becca, Russell thanked his lucky stars, good parenting and common sense from the part of his youngest. Twice a year Peter had held gatherings and his family had met Dynamo numerous times. A few years ago, Dynamo had made a drunken pass at Becca. Russell was grateful she had recoiled in horror. "I thought I was being nice." Russell put on his poker face. "It's not like I said I hoped he would crash his sports car into a telephone pole."

Becca giggled. "Come on dad, you're really close to retiring. Then you won't have to see Dynamo anymore." He felt the grin in her voice. "Pretty soon you and mom will take a long European vacation. But you had better lose weight if you plan on keeping up with her down those cobblestone streets."

Russell peered quickly at his grinning daughter then looked back at the congested road ahead of him. Just how much had his three women been planning for him so far in advance? They were prone to ridiculous fancies which had him footing the bill for outrageous trips. Like huffing up to Machu Pichu, roaming around dilapidated stone ruins in England and bouncing around a safari jeep in Tanzania. Apparently, he would soon be trapsing around Europe. What was the problem with taking in a some shows in Vegas like normal folk? He sighed. "Alright, Becks. I promise I'll start walking."

He felt her dubious stare on the side of his head. "Uh-huh. I'll talk to mom about it."

***

Saturday morning was lazy breakfast day for Heather and Russell. He woke up to the light filtering around the heavy drapes and rolled over on his side. He sat up, stretched and yawned before giving Heather a little shake. She responded with an unintelligible mumble as he winced to his feet. He dragged his feet to the door, unhooked his robe and shuffled across the hall, down the stairs and into the foyer. He yawned and stretched one arm overhead before he opened the front door and bent to pick up the paper with a grimace. Russell still liked to read a newspaper but his favourite publication had thinned over the years and was now only available on the weekends.

Russell doddered back into the kitchen, tossed the newspaper on the table and started the coffee machine. He set out a bowl and spoon for himself and a plate with a butter knife for Heather. He yawned dramatically and turned to rummage in the pantry. He pulled out the sugary weekend cereal for himself and the bland, cardboard sliced bread that Heather favoured. Russell looked up as his sleepy wife padded into the kitchen and gave him a kiss before opening the fridge door to fumble out the milk. Russell set down their steaming mugs of coffee as Heather walked over to the toaster with two slices of bread in hand.

"Hon? Is something wrong?" Heather gave him a cockeyed look. "You've got something on your mind."

Russell looked up from his mug. "Becca's still sleeping?"

Heather nodded. "I think I heard her get in at four in the morning. I'll wake her if she's not up by lunchtime." She gasped and blew on her hands as she grabbed the steaming toast. "What's on your mind?"

"You remember I was talking about the Boxen Industries proposal yesterday at dinner?" Russell asked.

"Yes, you said it went well." Heather walked to the kitchen table and dropped her toast on the plate. "You think maybe you won't get the sale?"

"No, it's not that." Russell sighed. "Well, I mean, maybe we won't get the sale because of something I said."

Heather pushed back a stray blonde lock and gave him a quizzical look. "What did you say that could have ruined it?"

Russell searched for the right words, then gave up. "Apparently I told Hector Wallace to go fuck himself."

Heather's eye dilated and she put a hand to her mouth. "What?"

"Yeah. I know." Russell put his hands on his smooth head and gave Heather a sheepish look. "I don't even remember it, Hezzy. I'll tell you my part and then what Cathy and Mark told me." Russell heaved in a breath and then launched into the conversation with Mark and Cathy before the meeting. He gave as many details as he could remember to describe the successful meeting itself with Boxen Industries. He explained how even Wallace seemed please, especially when Russell had promised him a free upgrade which Cathy and Mark weren't too happy about. He said it had all gone well, until he said his goodbyes. Russell told Heather he had no memory at all of telling Wallace off. If he hadn't had seen Mark and Cathy so upset he would have thought it was a joke.

Heather gave him encouraging nods until he finished. "Wow. I'm sorry honey-bear."

Russell tapped his spoon hard on the table. "I damned near screwed it up. Cathy smoothed things over with Wallace." He sighed. "Are you mad at me?"

Heather raised an eyebrow. "Mad? Why would I be mad? I agree with Cathy. You are probably just stressed out. You've been overloaded with responsibilities since Peter died." She bit into her cold toast. "And now with Dynamo in the picture it's just gotten worse."

Russell stared into his coffee. "Yeah, that's probably all it was." He shook his head. "It's just so weird that I really can't remember it."

"It's like a mild, post-traumatic stress. Your mind is blocking it out." She squeezed his hand. "Don't you remember the Blather documentary about it?"

Russell grimaced "Is there a Blather documentary for everything?"

Heather chuckled. "Yes, there is!" She cleared off the plates. "Come on, don't be a Gloomy Gus." She gave him a mischievous grin. "You can take your mind off it by driving Becca and I to the mall for lunch."

Russell smiled. "Sounds like a wonderful idea."

Chapter 5: It was only a dream:

The greenish tint caused Russell to cringe. He looked around his bedroom and saw the same scene as the first dream. The colours were off, the furniture size wasn't right, and Heather and sleeping-Russell were snug in their now king size bed. He looked at the drapes and saw them closed. They looked heavy. Somehow the mind-itch told him with an 'X' that it was pointless. No matter how hard he tried, he wouldn't have the strength to draw them open.

With a noisy sigh Russell padded to the center of the bedroom and crossed his arms. He frowned. Why the wait? True, the last dream also had him waiting. Technically speaking, of course. In the first dream he had no idea that Gizmo would appear, so it was difficult to say he was made to wait. But now he was pretty damned sure Gizmo would show up in this dream. So why wouldn't his mind just hurry up? If he knew what was going to happen, why didn't it just happen? The alternative answer was far worse. Russell refused to believe the other dimension nonsense. There was no such thing. Period. This was a dream, not an alien encounter.

A bizarre idea bloomed in Russell's mind. Was it his own brain that was deliberately making him wait? Other than the myriads of UFO, alien, alternate dimension, multiverses, psychic and demonology Blather documentaries, Heather had made him watch shows on dream psychology. So, it was reasonable to assume that his inner self was trying to say something to his—what? Outer self? Or to his Id? Or maybe to the ego? Heather had shown him an iceberg diagram about human consciousness, but for the life of him he couldn't remember what was above the waterline. If only he had paid attention.

Then he felt it. A very slight vibration under the rug. Russell gave himself a self-satisfied smile. He had outfoxed himself. All it took was some analytical thinking and he forced his mind to bend to his will. It made sense. After all, it was his mind and he wouldn't let it run roughshod over himself twice. This time he would face his Id-ego and give it a piece of his mind, so to speak. And soon, because the roar was becoming deafening and he was blinded by the harsh, green light.

"Russell-human, we have returned." Gizmo loomed over him. He hadn't changed his cloak. Russell had changed his pajamas. What did that say about them?

"Yeah, Gizmo, I can see that." Russell gave him a smug grin. "I think I know what this is all about."

"Russell-human, we are pleased that this you understands." The green bean offered a slow blink of praise. "It will make the un-restraining process of that other you much quicker."

"Right. Restraints." Russell pulled on his lip. "I think Cathy was the first to pick up on it. I'm under a lot of stress. For all intents and purposes, I'm the acting CEO. That drughead Dynamo certainly can't manage the company." He beamed his deal-closing smile. "Thanks for the help, Gizmo. This Id-ego thing has worked brilliantly. I just need to relax, share some of the responsibilities with Mark and Cathy and tell Dynamo to go back to Blunt University." He waved his hand. "I'm all set. You can go now."

Gizmo gave him a stupefied blink. "Russell-human, you have not understood as we willed you to."

Russell frowned. "Sure, I did. I just told you. I'm stressed"

"Russell-human, this you is dangerously dull-witted. We had hoped for better. We sifted through 1e-11 parallel universes to find this you. We observed this you for countless dream cycles. This you was the best we could find in order to reach that other you." Gizmo gave him a hard, fishy stare. "That you is considerably more acute. This you is an obtuse angle."

Russell narrowed his eyes. He was a successful business man. He made millions for his company. Who did the green bean think he was talking to? Russell really wasn't sure anymore. "Which me are you trying to reach? This me, or that me? When I wake up, which me am

I?" If Heather had heard him, he would find himself smothered in a Blather-world of documentaries.

"Russell-human, your mind is stagnant." This time the green bean curled his fish-lips. "We have explained this numerous times. We are using this you to reach that you. That you is more acute and will make better super-Russell-humans. When harnessed, that you will have enough potential mind to power a nuclear reactor." Gizmo sneered and pointed a long arm at Russell. "This you will be unlikely to toast bread."

"Listen, I've had enough." Russell waved his arms and squared his bare feet on the carpet. "Gizmo, we've identified the problem. We have our plan. Now I need to put the plan into action. Full stop." Russell pointed to the draped windows because he really wasn't sure where else to point. "You can leave now."

"Russell-human, you have no power to invite us to leave. We have brought this you here to harness the energy of that you."

"I really don't understand."

"Russell-human, we have already explained this to you. You are you, but not that you. We need you to reach that you which is you though it is not you."

Russell felt like he was swimming in a circle with land nowhere in sight. "But why"?

"Russell-human, you are less cognizant than we believed." The green bean seemed disgusted. Or possibly saddened. The featureless faced was a tough read. Gizmo's fish lips wobbled. "We are lifting your restraints, Russell-human. But we fear only that you will succeed."

"My name is Russell. Just Russell."

Gizmo began to glow and the room trembled violently. "Just-Russell-human, heed our words! Your restraints will be lifted further! The time is near! You will give rise to a new species of ultra-unrestrained Just-Russell-superhumans!"

***

"Russ? Russell! The alarm has been going off for a minute!"

Russell moaned into his pillow. "What"?

He heard Heather's feet pad around the bed. Russell opened an eye to see her frowning face inches from his own. She put her forehead to his. "You don't have a fever." Heather pulled back suddenly. "You had the dream again, didn't you?"

Russell closed his eyes. "Just give me a few minutes, Hezzy."

"No! Roll over." She pushed and shoved him over on his back. "Stop being a baby and open your eyes."

"I'm awake." Russell was met by her grinning face.

"So, tell me about it." Heather rocked her hand on his chest. "Was it the same dream?"

"Hon, I don't remember." Russell thought for a moment. He really couldn't remember.

Heather stood up straight, crossed her arms and narrowed her eyes. Even though Russell couldn't see below her knees, he knew she was tapping her foot. "Well, think about it. If you think hard, it will come back to you. But do it right away or you'll lose it."

"Hez, who cares?"

"I care! Dreams are important." Heather pursed her lips. "Hurry up or you'll be late for work. Coffee's on."

Russell watched her pad out of the room. He looked at the ceiling, squinted and searched his thoughts. He really couldn't remember his dream. Russell grimaced when he realized he would be able to bring it to mind if he looked into the vanity mirror like last time. He would have refused the idea, but it was rather pointless. Sooner or later, he would need to see his reflection to shave. Unless he decided to become a prophet.

With a push and roll Russell swung his feet to the floor. He tested his knee. It seemed less tender. He still winced a little as he stood, but it wasn't as bad as the other days. He patted his belly and padded to the side of the vanity. He kept his eyes closed and waited. Slowly, he opened his eyelids and peered into the mirror. He was hit with a flash that took his breath away. There was a sudden rush of colours and images so vivid for a moment he thought the green bean was standing in front of him. *Dammit*, he thought. Gizmo had indeed visited him last night. No, his Id-ego mind had invented Gizmo because he was stressed. That was better. That was logical. Except he couldn't explain why the mirror triggered the memories. Were mirror's a gateway to other dimensions? He was curious but knew better than to ask Heather.

Russell heard Heather's call waft up to the bedroom. He groaned silently and reached for his robe. He took a moment to mentally prepare to be grilled under the hot lights of Heather's gaze. With a plod and wince, he left his safe room and slowly walked down the hall. He paused at the stairs and listened to Heather's happy clinking and humming. As quite as a mouse, Russell tiptoed down the stairs, touching the ground floor lightly and shuffled into the kitchen. He was immediately accosted by Heather's stare.

"You remembered the dream!"

"No, I didn't."

"Yes, you did, honey-bear!" She grinned as she set the coffee mugs on the table. "You can't fool me."

Russell sighed as he poured his cereal into his favourite bowl. "What does it matter? It's only a dream."

Heather sipped her coffee. "Maybe. Or maybe you were visited by an interdimensional being."

Russell rolled his eyes. "There's no such thing."

"Yes, there is! How many times have we watched the quantum reality Blather documentaries?" She took a bite of her bone-dry toast. "It's science."

"It's not science." Russell poured in too much milk and frowned. "Those are just wacky theories invented by pseudo-scientists so they can improve their Blather ratings."

"There are all kinds of cosmologists who believe it." Heather treated him to a wild, mischievous grin. "I believe it. You were visited by an alien from another dimension. It's so exciting!"

Russell cursed silently into his mug. He filled his mouth full of cereal and mumbled. "It's not exciting."

"So?" She raised an eyebrow. "What did Gizmo say?"

"The same thing. You know, the 'un-restraining' nonsense."

Heather looked at Russell. Her lips moved and suddenly her eyes widened and mouth dropped open. Russell knew what she was going to say. He hoped she wouldn't, but then she did. "Russ! Oh, my goodness! The alien lifted your inhibitions! You really were visited!" She clapped her hands. "That's why you told off Wallace! The alien switched off your filters!"

"Hezzy, no. That's ridiculous."

Heather pointed an accusing finger. Or maybe it was a triumphant finger. "You were thinking it too!"

"No, I wasn't." Deny the evidence, Russell thought.

"Yes, you were!" Heather chortled. "I know you too well, honey-bear!"

Russell grimaced. "It's impossible."

"Why is it impossible?" She sat down next to him. "Don't you remember all those Blather documentaries we watched on alternate dimensions and the multiverse?"

"No."

"Well, I do." She chuckled. "You had an experience with another world!"

"No, I didn't."

"This is so exciting!" Heather stood up. "I'm going to wake Becca."

"No!" Russell nearly spilled his coffee. "Please, Hezzy. Please don't tell her."

Heather frowned. "Why not?"

"Because it's crazy." He thrust out his chin. "And because I'm her father."

Heather stopped at the kitchen framed opening and turned. "What does that mean?"

Russell pondered. He wasn't sure, but if he said it, it had to mean something. "Just don't, ok. Let me just try to puzzle it through for a minute."

"I'm already done puzzling it through." Heather's eyes twinkled. "Can I wake Becca now?"

Russell raised a hand. "No, Heather, I'm serious." He gave her his most authentic, desperate look. "How about this; let's just see how it goes and then we'll decide together? But for now, please don't say anything."

Heather sighed walked back and kissed him on the head. "Ok, but you've only got until lunchtime the think and then I'm telling Becca."

Russell groaned softly as Heather chuckled into his neck.

***

Just as the board of director's meeting was set to start, Cathy dropped the bomb. It had been rescheduled in the afternoon to accommodate Dynamo. There were a few bewildered looks followed by an embarrassed silence. Cathy flushed red and stammered out that Dynamo had called her yesterday evening to let her know that he had an engagement in the morning that he couldn't miss. When Russell asked if Dynamo was meeting with his pusher, he got a black look from Cathy and a frown from Mark. He put up his hands, mumbled out a few curses to the room and stood up. Russell walked out of the board room shaking his head.

With a violent push Russell careened into his office and slammed the door. He ignored his knee and stomped to his desk and he threw his weight into his chair which creaked in protest. He picked up his calendar and cursed under his breath. He had two teleconferences this afternoon that he knew he would have to cancel. Who knew what 'afternoon' meant to Dynamo. It could be two o'clock, it could be four o'clock. If the brat showed up at five o'clock, he would ring his neck. Russell started typing the first email to excuse himself to his client and ask to reschedule. He had just sent the first email when there was a knock on his door and Mark walked in.

"Listen Russ, we're all upset, but you shouldn't have walked out on us." Mark folded his hands and stood in front of the desk.

Russell snapped his head up and scowled. "The meeting was rescheduled because the junkie is on a power trip."

"Yeah, I know." Mark sat down across from Russell. "But Cathy, John, Charlotte and I had a chat." He cleared his throat. "You know. To try to understand how to reach Dynamo."

Russell put his elbows on his desk. "Reach Dynamo? If by that you mean how to talk to the brat, it's easy. We tell him there are corporate rules and customs. The Board of Directors meeting is from eleven o'clock until twelve o'clock every week, just like it's always been."

"Yeah, I know." Mark tapped crossed his legs. "But Dynamo is the CEO now."

"And that means that he can reschedule without even giving an exact meeting time?" Russell didn't want his voice to be harsh, but he couldn't supress his angry tone. "What that kid needs is a lesson in discipline and respect."

Mark nodded. "True, but we need to know how to approach him. We can't talk to him like we used to talk to Peter."

"No, Mark, we didn't talk to Peter." Russell snapped. "We had discussions with Peter based on respect, common goals and knowledge on how to run a business." Russell felt his blood race. "We didn't bow to his every whim because there was no need to. We were all on the same wavelength."

Mark was silent for a few moments, then he sighed. "I know Russ. I know you're right, but things have changed."

"No, Mark, things haven't changed, they've gotten worse." Russell leaned back and took a deep breath. "Pandering to Dynamo will only make things worse still. We need to draw the line and he needs to learn to respect us. He has nothing to teach and everything to learn."

"I'll try to talk to Cathy about it."

"Yeah, please do that."

Mark nodded, gave Russell and embarrassed smile and stood up. "As soon as we know the BOD meeting time, we'll let you know."

"Sure." Russell turned back to his computer screen and pointedly ignored Mark as he left his office. Russell copied and pasted his first email into the body of the second, changed the names, title and company and hit send. He leaned back into his office chair, grabbed his tie and shook it wildly until it came loose. Russell looked at Cathy's strategic marking map and formulated some new offers. When Mark popped back in asking if he would join them for lunch, he snapped that he was busy and ordered himself a hero sub through Denise. After a heartburn filled lunch and images of Becca scolding him, Russell went back to formulating offers based on Cathy's strategy reports until he heard three, crisp knocks.

Russell called out. "Come on in, Cath."

Cathy opened the door and smiled. "You recognized my knock?"

"Sort of. The others call me on my desk phone and Mark pretty much charges right in as he knocks." Russell smiled. "So, it was pretty easy detective work."

Cathy's face turned suddenly sombre. "Dynamo has arrived and he walked straight into the board room. He said he's ready to begin the meeting."

Russell looked at his watch. It was ten to four. "Our drug czar is just in time for tea and crumpets."

"Russell, please." Cathy's entire being suddenly took on a bedraggled look. "He's our CEO and he is trying to indicate a new direction for Rave2Engrave."

"Right off a cliff."

"He might have some fresh ideas that only young people have." Cathy insisted. "So, the least we can do is collaborate."

"No, Cath, that's the most we can do with the likes of that junkie." Russell pursed his lips and snorted. "I'll be there in just a minute."

Cathy had her hand on the door. "Of course. We're all in the board room. Except John who is printing off the production figures. But he'll be there too. In a minute. So. Well. As soon as you can." Cathy stumbled out as she shut the door.

Russell picked up a pen and tapped it against his notepad cover. He looked at the purple lettering on the pink fluorescent background. '*Rave with Rave2Engrave*'. What could that slogan possibly mean? For a moment Russell seriously considered not going to the meeting. He wasn't afraid of disciplinary action, but with two years left before he retired his time could be relatively smooth, or a battle of headbutting rams.

The garish notepad seemed to taunt him. Would it make any sense to bring it? Probably not, but if Dynamo watched him walk in empty handed, he might take it as a slight. Assuming he was bright enough to put two and two together. Russell felt torn between confrontation and surrendering to the new management. He could throw in the towel and let Dynamo handle company strategy and profitability, but how long would the company last? Rave2Engrave was not a major player in the market and managed to thrive by taking calculated risks.

With a mighty sigh, Russell swept his notepad and favorite fountain pen off his desk. He winced as his knee adjusted to his swift strides to the door. He paused to shut out the lights and closed the door lightly behind himself. He stopped long enough to look at his plaque and glared down the hall at Dynamo's corner office. With heavy steps Russell walked to the sunny meeting room.

"Good afternoon, team." Russell nodded and sat down at the opposite end from Dynamo.

"Great," Cathy said. "We are ready to begin. Our first order of business is the company's actual output versus our estimated growth assessment over the last quarter. We looked at my estimates in our last meeting so we need to compare them with volumes." She looked up at the Production Manager. "John, could you give us the real numbers, please?"

"Cath, that sounds great," Dynamo interjected. "I mean, I know we need to go over the dry stuff too, but what about our passion?"

Cathy turned a worrying shade of pink. "What do you mean, Dynamo?"

"I mean—just hang on a second, Cath." Dynamo lifted a finger then picked up his gigantic monogrammed smartphone off the table, gave the screen a couple of swipes and put it to his ear. He winked at Cathy. "Hey Liv, it's me. Could you bring in the thumb drive with my new initiative? Great babe. Love you, too." Dynamo set down the phone and smiled at the petrified directors. "Livy will be with us in just a minute. Trust me, it's worth the wait."

Cathy made a strangled sound and nodded. Russell watched her avoid his gaze and she turned to look at John to whom she offered a grimace and a shrug. Russell cast a gaze at John who also studiously avoided him. Russell swivelled his chair towards Mark who was looking out the window. In a last heroic attempt, Russell looked at Charlotte. She did meet his gaze, but seemed to wilt a millisecond later. With no one else to run through the visual wringer, Russell turned to Dynamo. Dynamo met his stare and did not turn away. Russell heard his blood pump through his ears as he watched Dynamo sneer.

"Good afternoon, everyone! I'm so glad Dynamo called me to participate!" In strutted Olivia Johnson, Dynamo's half English, half Spanish find from who-knows-where. Russell watched the painted doll click across the floor on ridiculously high heels and an obscenely short skirt. He cringed at the thought of his wife witnessing the spectacle. If Heather saw Olivia sache into a boardroom dressed like that she would knock her over with a backhand. Russell considered the marketing assistant with her long dark hair, almond eyes and full figure. She could have been a beautiful young woman, if she hadn't been so fawningly crass. Her coy stares at the leering Dynamo were stomach turning. Russell had no idea if Olivia possessed any real talent, but her willingness to obey the junkie's whims was undoing years of Cathy's strategic marketing work in a matter of months.

"Looks, great Liv. I love the colours." Dynamo gave the giggling Olivia a wink. Russell thanked the gods of good sense that he didn't swat her backside. Dynamo swiped his tablet and to the chagrin of the directors his presentation was displayed. It was entitled '*A Vision of the Hereafter*'. Russell couldn't be sure if it was a play on words or if the title had been thought up under the influence of magic mushrooms. Dynamo gave Olivia one final ogle. "Ladies and gentlemen, let me welcome you to the future of Rave2Engrave." He swiped to the next slide. "Welcome to Rave2Space! Our bold new mission is manned space flight!"

Staring at everyone from the large monitor was a smiling Dynamo superimposed into a sci-fi space suit. In the background, what could only be described as a nineteen fifties cartoon rocket blended together with a futuristic flying saucer with the Rave2Space purple and pink logo. Russell would have burst out laughing if he hadn't see the company sinking in his mind's eye. Dynamo had really planned on making the buffoonery in the Mission Statement come true. The junkie bobbed in his plush office chair. "Wow. It gives me goosebumps to think about it." He winked at Olivia. "How about you Liv?"

Olivia giggled, "I can't wait to be on board to feel the good vibrations!"

The buffoons peeled with laughter as Cathy tried to intercede. "Dynamo, what is this? We don't have the funds nor the knowledge for such a venture."

"Cath. Cathy!" Dynamo shook his head. "We don't have the money or the engineer skills today, I know that. But this is our *Hereafter.*" He swiped back to the presentation title screen. "We need to plan for the future and we need to plan big. Cath, you don't want Rave2Engrave to be left behind, do you?"

"Left behind?" Cathy mumbled. "Dynamo, we make engraved rollers and conveyor belts."

"That's today, but what about tomorrow?" Dynamo swiped the presentation forward. "Everyone knows the future is on Mars. We'll probably have killed the planet in fifty or so years, so we might as well just get off it. Right?"

"Right!" Olivia squealed.

Russell looked away from Dynamo and bore his gaze into Mark, willing him to speak. The engineering manager turned a despicable shade of red as he looked back at Russell. Mark licked his lips. "Dynamo, I've been a mechanical engineer for nearly thirty years. What you are talking about is so far out of our scope that there is no way for us to bridge the technological divide." He loosened his tie. "And that doesn't even begin to consider the resources that would be necessary to finance the hiring of personnel, laboratories, specialized drafting and software programmes, and the like."

"Mark, didn't NASA put a man on the moon ten years after Kennedy announced it?" Dynamo leaned back in his chair and threaded his fingers behind his head. "Where there's a will, there's a way."

"Dynamo, NASA was funded with billions of dollars." Mark was sweating visibly. "We don't even have the budget to design a fastener fit for space."

"Mark, my man," Dynamo shook his fist. "Isn't that the perfect first step? We get into the game designing space-worthy nuts and bolts. Then a rocket engine. Then the whole ship." He smiled at the melting engineering director. "What do you say, chief? Can I count on you to kick-off the design process?"

Mark slurred, "Well, I—I think. Maybe on a slower day I could look at—"

"Great!" Dynamo winked at Olivia. "Didn't I tell you we had a great team?"

"You sure did!" Olivia gushed.

"We just need to budget, right Charlotte?" Dynamo half-spun his chair to face the Chief Financial Officer. "Can you do some number crunching for me, Charlie?" Though Charlotte was the youngest of the board of directors, Russell thought she might have a stroke. Her eyes twitched and she managed a nod. The junkie's eyes were afire. "This is looking promising. Very promising." Russell watched as Dynamo turned to him, a look of challenge in his eyes. "That only leaves us to find clients. Russ, my man. What does our salesman say?"

"What do you suggest, Dynamo?" Russell kept his eyes trained on his fountain pen for a moment. He drew a breakth then he looked up to meet Dynamo's gaze. "Should I call NASA and ask to speak to an astronaut?"

Dynamo barked out a harsh laugh. "Funny, Russ." He wagged a finger, then crossed his arms. "No, I was thinking smaller. You know, some sub-suppliers in the industry. You could offer our services to make some of the less critical parts. Then we can work our way up from there." Dynamo gave him a cold look. "Can I count on you, Russ?"

Russell felt all eyes on him. It was do or die. In an instant Russell thought what he should do and then decided he wasn't going to die for it. "Of course, Dynamo."

"Wonderful!" Dynamo nearly leapt from his seat. "Livy, didn't I tell you they were great?"

"You surc did, Dyna!"

"Yeah, they are great." Dynamo clapped his hands together. "Well, I think the rest of the points can wait until tomorrow. Or the day after.

I want my team out there like aggressive tigers! I want you guys to make *Mission Rave2Space* happen! Out you go!" He waved them to the door. "Let me see you aggressive! Let me hear you roar!"

"Sure thing! Let me crunch numbers! I'll work with Olivia! The design team will be hyped! You're a crackhead who's going to sink our company! Marketing will do its part! We're on it!" The directors filed out of the boardroom, Russell leading the retreat. He retraced his steps angrily, clomping down hard despite his protesting knee. He stopped in front of his office and drew in a deep breath. He jerked open the door, limped inside and closed it with a little too much force. Russell glanced at his desk, then limped to the left and threw himself on the low, cushy loveseat with a small coffee table and plump, low chairs that he used for relaxed late meetings with Cathy and Mark.

The farce of the board of directors meeting tumbled over in his mind. When had they lost control of the situation with Dynamo? To Russell, the junkie's hands on the helm seemed sudden, but was it as sudden as it seemed? He thought back to comments over the past months by Cathy and Mark. If he had to be honest, his two experienced lieutenants did try to convey to him that Dynamo was more present and engaged. The junkie was always late, never concentrated on the task at hand, but he was in the office often enough voicing his opinion. Russell by and large ignored him and continued to work at his job and took the leadership role that Peter had. He realized that he hadn't noticed that Dynamo was seizing power from him. Russell had simply treated him like a drugged-up nuisance and hadn't clued into the fact that Dynamo was charging up behind him.

The door flew open to a frantic Mark, his thinning hair plastered to his head by bucketload of sweat. "Fuck, Russ! Why did you have to say that?"

Russell uncrossed his legs and sat up. "What's the problem? I said I would participate." He shook his head. "Not that I actually will. I'll figure a way around the junkie's psychotic space race."

"No Russ, I'm talking about what you said as we were leaving the boardroom." Mark sat down heavily on the cushy chair. "You called Dynamo a junkie who's going to destroy Rave2Engrave!"

Russell blinked. "I said that?"

"Yeah, Russ." Mark held his gaze. Russell saw there was no humor in his eyes. "You really did."

Russell shook his head. He had thought of shouting at Dynamo. He always thought about calling him a useless junkie. But he was certain he hadn't said it out loud. "You're sure I said that?"

Mark leaned back and covered his face with his hands. "Russ, please. Do you want me to call Cathy?" He waved a hand. "Don't worry. As soon as she's done convincing Dynamo that you were only joking, I'm sure she'll kick down your door and strangle you with your tie."

Russell nodded and wiped his eyes. He looked at Mark who shook his head and slouched back into his seat. Russell thought back to the meeting. It had only ended minutes ago. He could remember every absurd moment right until the end. He could still feel his shock when he realized that the new Mission Statement wasn't a flight of fancy, but a descent into madness. He vividly remembered his blood boiling when Dynamo called upon him to be part of the farce. He remembered agreeing to it. He got up and left. That was it.

There was a panicked woodpecker thrum at the door. "Cathy, come in!" Mark and Russell's chorus was more frantic than her knock.

"Russ! Russell!" Cathy was beside herself. Her eyes were swollen. Her face was red. Her pallor was that of a vampire in the long Norwegian winter. She trembled violently. "Why Russ? Why did you have to say it?"

Russell pushed himself onto his feet with a wince. He walked over to the small counter. "Cath, please sit." He poured three glasses of water, set them on a tray and limped back to the coffee table. Mark grabbed two glasses and set them down. Cathy had drained her glass before Russell had even slouched into the loveseat.

"Russell, what's going on with you?" Cathy sniffled. "Is there something you aren't telling us?"

"Yeah, Russ." Mark gripped his shoulder. "Is it the stress of doing Peter's job? I know you're not happy about Dynamo stepping in, but maybe you could let him take some of the workload."

"Exactly, Russ." Cathy chimed in. "Under your guidance maybe you can ground him. Show him how to run a company and just worry about sales."

Russell looked back and forth. "You both understand the direction Dynamo suggested our company should take in the future, right?"

Mark sighed. "Fine. We know it's a crazy idea, but Cathy and I are certain he'll grow out of it." He grimaced. "But we have to remember it's technically his company."

Cathy gulped from Russell's glass and wiped her mouth. "Yes, it's his but he needs help. He's going through a teething phase."

"So, you admit he's a spoiled brat?" Russell felt his arteries pulse. "A baby who will destroy what we've worked for?"

Cathy folded her hands. "Russell, please. I think you're overreacting."

"You think I'm overreacting?" Russell shifted angrily in the chair. "Cathy, if we even start this plan rolling when our clients get wind of it, they'll jump ship. The Germans won't even let us in the door."

Mark put a hand on his arm. "Russ, we can just put forward a plan that even Dynamo will realize is impossible to bring forward. Come on, he's not stupid."

"That Vision Statement he presented is beyond stupid." Russell snapped. "It's foolhardy and reckless. It would literally destroy Rave Engraving."

"Rave2Engrave, Russ." Cathy put a hand on his arm. "Please, help him see that this plan is not viable. Dynamo never had a father growing up. Peter divorced his mother when he was only two years old and never really engaged with him again until he was a teen." Cathy gave him a pleading look. "He lacks a guide."

Russell sat back and let himself be enveloped by the armchair. He took a deep breath, then leaned forward, rested his elbow on his chin and put his chin in his hand. The three sat in silence and Russell pondered. He didn't doubt he called Dynamo a company wrecking junkie, but he wasn't sure if he was happy that he did. The last time he felt himself at a crossroads of this importance was when he convinced Peter many years ago to risk the company's future by branching out with a risky new endeavour. But he had been a younger man working with someone who understood business. Dynamo was not that man.

Chapter 6: Decoding Gizmo:

"What's up, honey-bear?" Heather peered over the counter as Russell set the table and Becca arranged their meal on the serving tray.

Russell carefully set down a fork. "Nothing, why?"

Heather raised an eyebrow and Becca gave him a playful smile. "You can't fool us, dad. We can read you like a book."

Russell always wondered how that was possible. He was the master of the business poker face. He could alter his expression in a client meeting in less than a blink of an eye to change the mood and close the sale. Then he came home and his poker face failed him miserably. He sighed. "There may have been another choice-word incident."

Becca and Heather exchanged looks as they brought the broiled meat and vegetables to the kitchen table, silent like stalking cats. Two sets of hazel eyes stared unblinkingly as he set down the last piece of cutlery. Russell grimaced and began to narrate the events of the morning, the hard words with Mark and Cathy, then the late start of the board meeting. He was secretly pleased to see the shock on their faces when he told them of Dynamo's space plan. Though Becca and Heather knew nothing of his industry, they were anything but stupid. Russell was also relieved when they didn't raise an eyebrow when he told them what Mark and Cathy claimed he said about Dynamo.

"Wow dad." Becca laid a couple of slices of roast in his plate. "That's the second time and you don't remember anything at all?"

"No, Becks, I really don't." Russell poured wine for his daughter.

"It could be the stress." Becca looked at Heather. "Mom, what do you think?"

Heather sipped her wine, her eyes dangerously close to betraying the worst. "Yeah, it could be stress." She set down her glass and Russell cringed. "Or maybe it could have been Gizmo."

"Hezzy, come on!" Russell pointed at Becca. "Your daughter is in the room!"

"Dad! What's that supposed to mean?" Becca looked from Russell to Heather. "Mom?"

"Becca, I have no idea what he means." She put a hand on Russell's forearm. "Russ, I'm just saying that maybe your dream was more than a dream."

"That's ridiculous." Russell slashed his meat. "You don't have a shred of proof that it was anything else."

"Except the odd fact that you can't remember uttering those shocking words." Heather said. "And both times it happened the day after a dream."

"Yeah, and mom said you can't remember the dreams right away, but they come to you afterwords." Becca chimed in. "That's really weird. Normally you remember dreams right away or you forget them." She looked at Heather. "Do you think there's a trigger? Like in the Blather documentary we saw about aliens planting thoughts and then the people discovered them under hypnosis?"

"Oh, that's right!" Heather nodded. "Then it could be that some word or event is triggering his memories shortly after to remember the dreams."

"And then some other cue is triggering dad's inhibitions filters." Becca added. "You know, so he can get things off his chest."

"You're right, it all makes sense!" Heather turned to Russell. "What do you think, Russ?"

Russell carefully pondered his words. "I think both of you are crazier than I am."

"Dad, come on! Just think about it rationally." Becca said.

"Your daughter's right." Heather bit into cauliflower. "It makes perfect sense."

"No, it doesn't!" Russell snapped. "It's stress."

"Well, honey-bear, you do seem stressed now." Heather looked at Becca who nodded. "We won't press the point. Becca's home, so let's just have a quiet dinner."

"Yeah, please." Russel poked through his vegetables. "Let's do just that."

The three lapsed into silence as Russell brooded. The dour mood didn't last long as Heather and Becca started up the conversation again, this time about Europe. In less than a minute the two were speaking excitedly about the couple's retirement trip to see the Eiffel tower, days wandering through the Louvre and D'Orsay, then a lazy drive to see Versailles. Russell felt his mood lighten just as he was certain so would his wallet, but he smiled at the chatter. He tried not to think of his next encounter with Dynamo, but sooner or later he would have to confront him.

***

The next day in the office was thankfully quiet with no client onsite. Russell closed himself in his office and zipped through email after email throughout the morning. His afternoon was jammed with back-to-back teleconferences which kept him in meetings for most of the day. To avoid having to eat with Mark and Cathy, he called up a client on the East Coast at lunchtime and deliberately let the meeting run long by chatting about golf and tennis. Dynamo didn't come in that day but Russell wasn't sure if he should read into it. The junkie didn't show up every day, and rarely did he announce his presence beforehand. Russell managed to plow through the day and left the office early, telling Denise he had a personal appointment. He had managed to put a buffer between himself and his colleagues for a day, but Dynamo was certainly around the corner.

Russell rolled out of the parking lot just as his car signaled his oldest daughter Michelle was calling. He pressed the button on his steering wheel to activate the Bluetooth receiver. "Russell Dymek esquire, world visionary speaking."

"Oh, that crazy Dynamo!" Michelle giggled. "Hey dad, how's it going?"

"Hi sweet-pea. All's well." Russell hit the wall of traffic merging on the Captain Blunt Expressway. "How's life in the Rockies?"

Michelle's tinny voice was suddenly loud and clear under the signal tower. "It's great, even though it's crazy expensive."

"Yeah, I know it from my business trips out West." Russell scowled as a car nearly cut him off. "Everything seems to cost a good thirty percent more."

"For sure. luckily Greg's job pays well," Michelle sighed. "Mine not so much."

"You only just started Micky." Russell put on his blinker and looked over his shoulder. "It'll take some time. You're a good worker; you'll probably get a bonus and maybe even a raise."

"Hopefully." There was a dreaded pause. "So, mom told me about your dream."

Russell shook his head. What was it about his girls? All three of them were obsessed with dreams. "Uh, yeah. A bit weird. No big deal."

"Mom says maybe it wasn't a dream."

Russell would have to speak with Heather before between his three women got him committed him to the looney bin. "It was just a dream, sweet-pea."

"But what if it wasn't?" Russell could hear Heather's stubborn insistence creep into Michelle's voice. "You remember those Blather documentaries about the multiverse?"

All three of them, he thought. All three were crazy and they were going to drag him down into the pit of madness. "It was just a dream, Micky. Not some other world encounter."

"Maybe a psychic would help." Michelle stated factually. "The real ones can contact the other realities, you know."

How his oldest daughter could graduate with a business degree and work as a strategic marketing manager yet believe such nonsense was a mystery. He sighed. "I'll think about it."

"I'm just trying to help, dad."

"I know, Michy." Russell looked over his shoulder and merged with oncoming traffic. "I'll talk to your mom about it, ok?"

"Ok! Well, I need to get back to work, but I'll talk to you soon." Russell heard a smack which he assumed was a kiss. "Love you, dad!"

"Love you, too." The line clicked and his car radio started back up with some seventies rock. The entire situation was getting out of hand, and his business sense was tingling, but not in a good way. There was no sale to be had, but there was a problem to solve. He would have to tell Heather there was nothing left to discuss. A dream was a dream and it was time to get back to real life. It was that simple. Tomorrow he would put his foot down and that was that.

***

Heather put two steaming mugs of coffee on the table. "Hey Russ, I was thinking."

Russell sighed and picked up his favourite mug. It was blue with a brilliant take on 'carpe diem'; *seize, but don't squeeze*. He looked across at Heather. "Please don't."

Her hazel eyes lasered him. "Maybe you should see a psychic."

Russell nearly choked on his coffee. "Absolutely not!" He tabled his accusation to an invisible judge. "You told Michelle about my dream and now you're both talking psychics!"

Heather frowned. "Yeah, so? What can it hurt? Who knows, maybe psychics can see into other dimensions."

"Hezzy, you don't really think that, do you?"

Heather bit her lip. "I'm undecided." She shrugged. "But maybe they aren't all fakes. The one Michelle went to really hit the nail on the head."

Russell put his head in his hands. Michelle had gone to a psychic several times when she was stressed out during exams at Blunt University. His oldest daughter had told him all about it, every last detail, but all he remembered was her fear of the future and wanted to know if she would one day be successful. Micky had said other things but Russell admitted they had gone in one ear and out the other. "The witch probably just guessed what would have been troubling a business student under exam pressure."

"Don't call the psychic a witch!" Heather punched him in the arm. "You don't know the first thing about her."

"And I plan on keeping it that way."

"Now, what was her name?" Heather walked to the fridge and began ruffling through the maze of magnets. "Here she is!" Heather triumphantly waved a violet business card. "Madame Amethyst!"

Russell snapped his head around. "What? Amethyst is a rock, not a name."

"Amethyst is technically quartz." She frowned. "And what's the problem with her name? My name is 'Heather', and heather is a plant. So why can't the psychic be named Amethyst?"

"Hezzy, please," Russell groaned. "It's not the same thing."

"Do you want me to call and book, or should we just drop by her place?"

"I'm not going."

"I'll book, she's probably very busy. Oh, I was just thinking!" Heather walked back to the kitchen table, picked up her cell phone and opened the Blather Search Engine. "We could speak with a UFO researcher!"

"No way, Hezzy!" Russell waved a finger. "I'm drawing the line. That's a no. N.O. No."

"There's one here in Blunt City. Oh, no way!" Heather looked up and grinned. "There are two of them! One is a physics professor at Blunt University specialized in the multiverse!" She chuckled. "I told you it was science!"

"The multiverse is pure fiction."

"Sometimes today's fiction is tomorrow's fact."

Russell knew when to throw in the towel.

Chapter 7: The Multiverse:

"Isn't this exciting?" Heather leaned into Russell.

"No, it's ridiculous." Russell was certain he was only one false step from being locked up. And then drugged up to the eyeballs. Maybe Dynamo would be an eventual cellmate.

"I think this is a really good idea." Heather hung on his arm. "And if Madame Amethyst doesn't help it's no big deal because in the afternoon we meet with Professor Singer."

Russell had lost. Big time. First, he had to see a witch masquerading as an oracle. And then he would be subjected to an institutional fraud of a university professor. His day was ruined. His life was ruined. He just as well should flush it all down the tubes. He was only two years away from early retirement but soon he would be in a straight jacket. "This is crazy, Hezzy. There is nothing either of them can do about my dream."

"But what if you really were contacted by an interdimensional alien?" She gave him a determined stare. "It really does happen, you know."

"How can you say that?" He balked. "Where's the proof?"

"You think all those people in the Blather documentaries are just making it up?"

"Yes."

Heather frowned. "That's not what you think."

"Half are liars and the other half are delusional." Russell set his jaw. "That's what I think."

She huffed. "Well, I don't think that."

"I know."

"Maybe some of them are liars." Heather pursed her lips. "And some of them really did seem delusional when they spoke on camera." She widened her eyes. "But wait! Remember the one about the two cops? They both saw the flying saucer crash and they both spoke with the alien!"

"They said the alien looked just like a man."

"The alien used mimicry to disguise itself."

"He was probably a dazed fighter pilot that was injured after he crashed the aircraft."

"The alien walked out of a UFO unscathed."

"A man walked out of a wreck."

"The alien described the future to them."

"A future so far away that we'll both be dead before it can be disproved."

Heather scowled. "You're a real spoilsport, you know that?"

Russell sighed. Why was Heather so deadest on proving the impossible? Why was she making such a fuss about nothing? "I'm not trying to be difficult, I just don't believe there are aliens or other dimensions."

"That's because you don't give them a chance."

Russell raised an eyebrow. "Aliens or dimensions?"

"Parallel universes, not dimensions." Heather rolled her eyes. "Anyway, give the aliens a chance."

"A chance to do what?"

"Reach out and talk to you." Heather shrugged. "You're one of the lucky ones you know."

Russell frowned. "Lucky how?"

"Most of the people visited are dragged off an experimented on." Heather raised her chin. "What do you think of that, Mr. Spoilsport?"

Russell couldn't find the loose of the knot to respond. It was only a dream. But in the dream Gizmo had done something to him. There was the pointing, the shaking, the sleeping-Russell, the 'X' over whatever he tried to do that the green bean didn't like. And the alien seemed to be able to make him drop off to sleep on command. That damned beanpole had all the power. "If there's another dream, I'm going to figure out how to shoot him. Tomorrow I'm buying a shotgun."

"No, you're not." She pointed at a neat white house with a covered porch and small yard with perfectly trimmed shrubs. "Look! Here we are, right on time." Heather grinned impishly and swept open her free arm. "Madame Amethyst awaits."

Russell stopped to ponder the sign. *Madame Amethyst: Psychic, Reader & Guide*. He frowned. What would she see, what would she read and where would she guide him to? He desperately wanted to turn and run but his aching knee would likely rebel after five paces giving Heather the chance to tackle him to the ground. He was certain the psychic's purple door led to madness. Russell sighed as Heather grinned and tugged at his arm. "Yeah, I'm coming."

"We have to ring the bell and wait." Heather pressed the button and distant windchimes sounded.

Russell cast a glance over his shoulder, yearning for the sidewalk of freedom. "Let's say we're Spaghettifarians so she'll turn us away."

"Hush!" Heather smiled as the door opened to reveal a middle-aged woman with long, salt and pepper hair wearing a subdued, earthy orange sweater and a long brown skirt. Other than an inordinate amount of wooden and crystal jewellery, Russell thought she looked normal. Heather gave a small wave. "Hello Madame Amythest. We're the Dymeks. Heather and Russell."

"Welcome." Madame Amythest folder her hands and gave something that looked halfway between a nod and a bow. "Please come in."

Heather plunged into the covered porch with Russell dragging behind her. Inside there was a small foyer where they took off their shoes and put on slippers from a shoe rack that held dozens of pairs. Russell tried to find fault with the eccentricity, but couldn't as it was a strict rule of Heather's, too. Slippers on, they followed the psychic to a large room in the back of the house where sunlight poured through the windows. Russell imagined a dark and purple place with skulls and pentagrams and wasn't sure if he was disappointed or relieved as they sat at a small, round table surrounded by house plants and only a few psychedelic wall hangings. Russell frowned at the crystal ball and candles on the table.

Madame Amethyst smiled and lit a candle. "How can I help you?"

"You can't, thanks for your time." Russell turned only to feel Heather's talons dig into his arm.

"My husband is a bit nervous." Heather didn't release her death grip. "He's a skeptic."

Madame Amethyst turned her soft gaze on Russell. "If you feel uncomfortable, Russell, you can reschedule for another time." She turned to Heather. "I think you understand, Heather, that we cannot force someone against his will."

"No, of course not." Heather took Russell's hand and gave him a warm smile. "Sorry for pushing you, Rus. We can go."

Russell looked at the two women and sighed. Somehow their few subtle words and actions had drained him of his will to fight. He would need to remember this for his next tough sales meeting. "No, it's fine. I just want it to be clear that I don't believe in any of this."

Madame Amythest took her seat at the table. "That's not a problem, Russell. What's important is that you come to me of your free will."

Russell nodded. "Ok, so how does this work?"

"However, you like," Madame Amythest said. "You can either tell me about your experience or I can conduct a reading."

Russell thought for a moment and figured it would be over quicker without obligating Madame Amythest into needless guesswork that he was certain she would get wrong. He sat with Heather at the table and began to tell her of his dreams, trying to included as many details as he could remember. For a moment he thought of twisting some details around to trap the psychic in the act of telling lies, but then he felt that was unfair. He never behaved that way with his clients and he always counted on mutual respect in any transaction. He kept all the details as true as he could remember them without embellishment. When Russell finished he had to admit he felt surprisingly relieved.

Madame Amythest smiled. "What is it that you would like to know?"

Russell shrugged, "nothing really. I think it's pretty clear."

"So do I," Madame Amythest said.

Heather gripped Russell's hand, "Madame Amythest, what does the alien want?"

The psychic took a moment then spoke. "I have been able to contact aliens from time to time, but I don't see one for Russell."

Heather frowned. "Are you sure? You see nothing at all?"

"I see someone standing over Russell." Madame Amethyst smiled. "But the man I see is not an alien."

Russell felt his hackles rise. "Let's just concentrate on my dream."

Heather turned. "We don't know if it's a dream. It could be contact." She turned to the medium. "Was it a dream?"

Madam Amethyst folded her hands. "Unfortunately, I can't be sure as I cannot contact this being, but it does seem to be Russell's subconscious speaking to him."

Heather frowned. "Really? No alien encounter?"

"It's not what I'm seeing. I do see a man trying to communicate with Russell but he is clearly a man." She paused. "Shall I continue?"

Russell had smiled when the psychic agreed that it was a dream, but now his smile quickly vanished. He looked at Heather who seemed to probe his mind. He cleared his throat. "Sure, by all means."

"The man is older than you, also without hair but has a short, white beard." She stared into her crystal ball, then back over Russell's shoulder. "Though he has not said as much, I believe he is the spirit of your father. He says his name is Paul. He also says he's very proud of you and believes you made the right decision years ago changing from your shared craft to your new career. Does this mean anything to you?"

Russell felt his mouth go dry as Heather dug her nails in deeper. For a moment he was at a complete loss for words. Then he shook his head and cleared his throat. "Yes, Paul Dymek was my father and he passed shortly after I changed my role in the company I work for." Russell rubbed his face and then smiled. "Madame Amythest, thank you, but I think we should be on our way."

Madame Amythest returned the smile. "Of course. It was a pleasure meeting you."

Heather was gaping and she looked back and forth. "Madame Amethyst, that was incredible! Thank you!"

They stood and Madame Amythest folded her hands and bowed. She accompanied them back to the porch where they traded slippers for shoes. Heather chatted relentless with Madame Amythest, thanking her for her insight and asked to book an appointment for herself the following week. The two women hugged and Russell offered an awkward wave. He exited the purple door with a jubilant Heather and walked down the short path and onto the sidewalk.

"Oh my goodness, Russ! She saw your father!" Heather grinned manically.

"Hezzy, she could have looked up my history online."

"Looked up what?" Heather frowned. "The obituaries? Then check at your Blather profile?"

"Exactly."

"Russ, I didn't tell Madame Amythest I was coming for Russell Dymek." She gave him a triumphant smile. "I booked with our first names only."

Russell turned this annoying fact over in his mind. How many Russells and Heathers coupled together could there be in city of three million? "Did you tell her that Michelle had seen her?"

"I only said I had been referred to by my daughter. I didn't give Madame Amythest's Michelle's name." Heather grinned up to her eyeballs. "Admit it, honey-bear, she got you good! And I always told you your dad would have been proud of your career change from accountant to salesman."

Russell continued to ponder. How had she known about his father who had been an accountant just like him? He must have said something in the conversation that made the psychic figure out who he was. Even if he worked in a niche market, he was a public persona. It would take only minutes to gather up data about him on the net. Russell thought that maybe the crystal ball was used to hide the psychic's phone. Madame Amethyst had put her hands behind it when Russell was telling his story. She could have used the time to conduct a Blather search.

As Russell thought about Madame Amethyst the magician, Heather chuckled gleefully as she got into the car.

***

The mathematics and science building was offset from the historical Blunt University where both Heather and Russell had studied years ago. The structure was a pre-millennial design, simple cement blocks and a glass atrium on the lower flower. Russell parked his car in the nearly empty lot and he walked with Heather along the concrete path into the main building. They stopped at front desk and announced themselves to the receptionist. They signed in to received badges and waited for professor Isaac Singer to meet with them. Russell perused the brochures until Heather darted towards a short, slight man about his own age with grey hair and thick rimmed glasses.

"Hello Professor Singer, I'm Heather Dymek and this is my husband, Russell." Heather smiled. "Thanks for taking the time, it's a real pleasure for us."

Singer returned the smile. "The pleasure is all mine, please follow me." Singer walked down the long corridor to a set of double doors. He pulled one open and motioned for the Heather and Russell to follow him up the stairs. They walked up one flight, then Singer stopped in front of the first door. Russell grimaced. An office by the stairs must have meant the fringe theory professor was small fish. He sighed and followed Heather into the office. It was a small space with one, large and cluttered desk with four chairs around it. There was nothing pinned on the walls save for a large white board with mathematical gibberish written on it and a small window which looked over the parking lot.

Singer motioned to the chairs in front of his desk. "Please have a seat. Can I offer you coffee or tea?"

"Oh, no thanks, Professor Singer" Heather smiled. "We don't want to take up much of your time, but we have some questions about my husband's alien visit from another universe."

"Heather," Russell groaned and gave Singer an embarrassed look.

Singer turned to Russell. "Well, why don't you tell me about it, Mr. Dymek."

Russell sighed. "It was just a dream."

Heather nudged him. "Russ, let the expert decide."

Russell fought hard not to roll his eyes and he tentatively began telling the tale with frequent prodding from Heather. He found it more difficult to explain the details to the professor than to the psychic and wondered if it was because he feared Singer would throw him out of his office. The tiny space meant to Russell he wasn't an important professor, but the scrawled equations on the whiteboard also told him the man was a professional in his field. In a few final fits and starts Russell finished the story. "And that's that, Professor Singer. As you can see, it was just a dream. Sorry if we're wasting your time."

"You're not wasting my time, Mr. Dymek, it's a fascinating account." Singer folded his hands. "May I ask you, did the being say how he reached our universe?"

Russell thought at the bizarre words of Gizmo. "No, he just appeared in a flash of light."

Heather nudged Russell. "Maybe you can ask him during the next visit?" She looked at the physicist. "Right, Professor Singer?"

Singer nodded. "I don't see why not." He angled his body towards Russell. "Did the being say he would return?"

Russell was silent for a moment then shook his head. "No, I don't think he did."

Singer folded his hands. "Mr. and Mrs. Dymek, I am employed as a theoretical physicist but I am also a researcher of the many worlds theory. The theory states that every possible combination is possible and there is a universe for each of these combinations." Singer stood, picked up a marker and walked to the whiteboard behind his desk. He rubbed out the equations with a small eraser. "There are many obstacles to our understanding of how the theory could be proved. We are trying to explain the universe bubbles and if they can come into contact with one another." He began to draw two universes on the whiteboard. "Another significant problem is we have no theoretical model to understand how it would be possible to travel between universes. Some have proposed entanglement."

Heather's eyes lit up. "What's entanglement?"

"You can think of it as quantum teleportation." Singer smiled. "But it's transporting information, not a physical object."

"Wow!" Heather grinned. "So, Gizmo teleported his conscious and Russell's into another universe?"

Singer raised an eyebrow. "That's an interesting hypothesis, Mrs. Dymek."

Heather chucked, "watch out or I'll take your job!"

Singer shared Heather's laugh while Russell imagined the three of them in separate padded rooms. Singer continued to draw and spoke over his shoulder. "Mr. Dymek, Gizmo said he was using you in order to communicate with a version of yourself in another universe. Did he explain why?"

Russell wasn't sure if he was more concerned about Heather theorizing science fiction into reality, or Singer using the green bean's dream name out loud. He rubbed his face. "No, he just said that other me was smarter."

"Well, Gizmo said more than that," Heather interjected. "He said he was going to lift your restraints and create a super-version of you." She smiled at Singer as Russell winced. "A version of super-Russells. It's so exciting the aliens picked my husband!"

Singer returned the smile. "It's extraordinary."

"And their plan is already working." Heather grimaced. "Even though it is awkward for Russell."

Singer raised an eyebrow. "They, or this one who speaks for many, has done something?"

Russell waved a finger. "No, he hasn't."

Heather put a silencing hand on his shoulder. "Yes, Gizmo has. He's loosening up Russell's inhibitions and causing him to speak out." She leaned on the desk. "And he doesn't even remember that he's said anything."

Russell was torn between speaking and hiding. The small office didn't present any secluded nooks. "I'm just under stress."

Heather frowned. "Well, maybe, but let's let the scientist decide." She turned back to Singer. "Professor, what do you think? Why has this alien species chosen Russell?"

Russell watched Singer's hand like a hawk. If it reached for a button under the desk he would run for the hills and drag Heather behind him. Instead, Singer spoke softly. "Mrs. Dymek, it's a fascinating story, though there aren't enough details for me to even hazard a guess."

"But Russell is telling the truth!" Heather folder her arms.

"I have no doubts," Singer nodded. "I firmly believe that the many worlds theory is plausible and that perhaps even contact between the worlds is possible, but there is no way to test it."

Russell frowned. "Then why do you believe it?"

"Fair question, Mr. Dymek." Singer lowered his marker and turned to face them. "Our universe, for all its power and complexity, was formed by a remarkable set of events after the Big Bang that allowed for a seemingly perfect balance. Without that balance perhaps life would never have come into being at all." Singer sat down at his desk. "It is thought that space-time did not, and does not, expand evenly, so it is possible that an infinite number of other universes formed with different physical laws."

"So," Heather flashed the physicist her mischievous grin. "It means that there could be another set of possibilities that form another balance and therefore other universes. Therefore, other Russells and Heathers could exist."

"Exactly, Mrs Dymek." Singer nodded. "That would be the idea behind the many worlds theory."

Russell shook his head. "Why would there be another me, then?"

"The theory states there could be countless versions of you." Singer replied.

Russell thought Singer sounded like Gizmo. Could this be a green bean conspiracy? "Professor Singer, is there another me or not?"

Heather frowned. "Russ!"

"It's fine, Mrs Dymek" Singer returned to the whiteboard and continued with his partially drawn multiverse. "It can be complicated and frustrating, especially considering we can't measure or even properly hypothesize the endless possibilities." He pointed to the whiteboard. "Here are some possibilities. As you can see, we have parallel universes that have the same laws, with different dimensions, a butterfly effect universe, or a universe that does not respect our mathematics. There could be another Russell Dymek, or not. If there is one, he might not be exactly the same because of circumstance or different physical laws after the Big Bang expansion. The possibilities are endless."

Heather nodded, enraptured. "But theoretically suppose there is another Russell, just like Gizmo said. Could Gizmo really have teleported his mind and Russell's into another universe?"

Singer spread his hands. "Assuming it was not a dream, perhaps Gizmo did exactly that."

Heather's eyebrows hit the roof. "Really?" She grinned at Russell. "Did you hear that, hon?"

"Oh yeah. I heard it, Hezzy" Madness was descending upon him. Was he still in time to escape it?

***

"I told you multiverse exists!" Heather looked smug as they walked back to the car.

Russell stopped and looked into her Hazel eyes. "Hezzy, did we attend the same meeting?"

"Well, of course Professor Singer's not going to come out and say it." Heather stated. "You have to read between the lines."

"The science is between the lines?"

"You've seen those Blather documentaries" Heather mimed a tablet with her hands. "They can never speak clearly or they'll be found out."

Russell frowned. "Found out by whom?"

"You know. The government. Secret agencies." Russell couldn't believe Heather actually seemed exasperated. "Rus, haven't you noticed in the Blather documentaries that a lot of the scientists and UFO abduction victims have to be interviewed in the shadows? And with voice overs?"

Russell understood where Michelles's stubborn insistence came from. He also realized his entire family was insane. "Heather, it was just a dream."

Heather set her jaw. "We'll see, honey-bear."

Chapter 8: Match Point:

Standing in his pale green bedroom in a fresh set of pajamas, Russell felt immersed in his third Gizmo dream. This time, he would take action. Or at least, he would try to. Russell wanted to pick up the baseball bat in the bedroom but the mind-itch stopped him as he was reaching under the bed. He hadn't bought a shotgun, but even if he had how could he use it in the dream? Maybe a video game shotgun would work. There were shooter games, so there must be guns for them. If there was a next time, he would be better prepared. For now, instead of clobbering or shooting Gizmo he would just have to give him a piece of his mind. It was better than nothing.

Under Russell's bare feet he felt the vibrations. They grew stronger as the walls began to shake. This time he was determined to take it all in to understand what was happening. He wouldn't close his eyes no matter how bright the light. Maybe if he was quick enough, he could tackle Gizmo just as he materialized. The sound in his ears became suddenly deafening. Russell fought to keep his hands by his side and his eyes open as the pale green light blinded him. He felt the scream in his ears and he clamped his hands over his head. When it all stopped, he cursed and looked up at Gizmo.

"Dammit Gizmo, what do you want from me?"

The green bean gave him a condescending look that only his fish lips and huge eyes could produce. "Just-Russell-human, this has been explained many times."

"You aren't making any sense!" Russell snapped. "What are you doing to me?"

Gizmo pointed at sleeping-Russell. "Just-Russell-human, that you is making tremendous progress. That you is able to harness his mind for telekinesis. That you can now communicate with us via telepathy." Russell thought he saw the green-bean frown as he pointed at him. "This you would have trouble stacking bricks in a light breeze."

Russell felt a catastrophic desire to strangle the green bean. But the damned "X" over Russell's hands around Gizmo's throat quenched his blood thirst. "If that me and this me are the same me, why is that me so much smarter?"

"Just-Russell-human, that you has applied himself to help lift his own restraints. This you is trapped because he refuses to open to the possibilities which that other you has now understood."

"Enough with the 'this you' and 'that you'!" Russell shouted. "And it's only Russell, ok? Only Russell, not 'just-Russell-human'.

"Only-not-just-Russell-Human, heed our words!" Gizmo raised his hand. Just as in the first two dreams, Gizmo began to glow and the bedroom blurred from the force of the quake. "This you's time has come to joint that you! Your restraints will be lifted even further! The time is near! You will begin a new species of ultra-unrestrained Only-not-just-Russell-superhumans!"

***

"Russ! Russell! Wake up! Come on, open your eyes!"

Russell groaned and slowly forced open his eyelids. He would have recoiled from Heather but he was buried in a sea of cushions while she sat on his chest like a succubus. He blinked. "What?"

Heather had a wide impish grin on her face. "You had the dream again!"

"No, I didn't," he grumbled.

"Oh yes you did, honey-bear" Heather chuckled. "It's the same scenario like the other times." She put her hands on her hips. "I wonder if we're caught in loop."

"Hezzy, I can't breathe."

"Sorry!" Heather slid off his chest and gave him a shove. "So? Are you going to tell me about it?"

"Hez, I don't remember a damned thing." Russel cringed as he thought of looking in the mirror. It was head shave day.

"I'm sure it'll come to you." She began tugging on his arm. "Now get out of bed and get right downstairs."

"Hon, you're going to make me fall on my face."

"Well, hurry up then!" She rustled to the door and unhooked her robe. "Come on! Coffee will be ready in a minute."

When will this end, Russell thought. It took him every once of will to push, pull and drag himself to his feet. He was pleased that his knee didn't protest. As stealthily as a panther he padded to the side of the mirror. He sidestepped in front of it with his eyes closed. He wondered if meditative breathing would help. Russell had joined Heather in a few of her yoga classes, and he thought he remembered enough. He slowed his breathing and imagined himself in a serene place. Vegas, the thought, taking in a Celine Dion show. He opened his eyes.

"Dammit!" Russell pitched forward and nearly knocked Heather's makeup off the vanity. The dream swirled around him, through him and over him. It was suddenly so vivid he there was no way to deny he had met Gizmo. But that was impossible. Aliens didn't exist and neither did other dimensions. With angry stomps he stormed into the bathroom, grabbed his electric razor and began to shave his head as he heard Heather calling him. He couldn't stomach the idea of cold coffee, so he renounced on shaving his face. With heavy steps he lumbered down the stairs and stopped in the door jam.

"You remembered!" Heather crowed.

"Hezzy, it's the same as the other dreams." Russell slouched into his chair.

Heather rushed over with two mugs and Russell poured his cereal. She plonked them down and gave him a shove. "So, what did Gizmo say?"

"The same things." Russell took a gulp of coffee. "Really hon, there was nothing new."

Heather's scrutinized him like an interrogator. "Did you ask Gizmo how he crossed universes?"

Russell cursed himself. As stupid as the entire situation was, it would have been a useful question. His mind couldn't have answered that question, so the entire affair would have been blown out of the water. "No, I didn't think of it." He sighed. "It's not easy to control a dream, you know."

"If it's a dream," Heather gave him a fisheye that looked suspiciously like Gizmo's stare. "Well, maybe you can ask him next time."

"There won't be a next time."

"How do you know?"

Russell didn't know. But he didn't know how to sell prototypes and yet he had figured that out. "I'll stop it from happening."

Heather frowned. "If you think it's a dream, and you have no practice in dreams, how do you think you'll stop it?"

Russell was stumped. He would seriously consider watching a Blather documentary if he could stop the green bean dream from ever happening again. "I don't know, and I'm late and I need to shave."

"Alright, but we're talking about it at dinner with Becca."

Russell grumbled as Heather grinned and rubbed her hands together.

***

Russell pulled up to his parking space just after 9:00 am. Lateness was something he frowned upon and he prided himself on his punctuality He always arrived before office hours and couldn't think of a time when he cam in late. He felt as though one of his tasks was to set an example that working hours needed to be respected by all, from the cleaner to the company owner. He caught himself sneering in the rearview mirror at the thought of the perpetually late Dynamo. Tomorrow he would show up an hour early and make the rounds in the workshop to speak with the production manager. It had been ages since he had done that and he could get in some walking that Becca was chiding him about.

Russell shook his had and opened the door, pleased to find that he didn't wince as his foot touched the ground.

The company atrium was bustling as Russell pushed through the glass door and walked the few steps to the front desk. He stopped in front of the secretary, tapped his watch and pointed to himself. She laughed and winked and he offered up a guild smile. Russell strode to the stairs and made his way up two steps at a time. He hummed tunelessly as he felt each step run through his bum knee with no pain. There was little more than slight ache that reminded him of where the pain had been. He reached the landing on his floor and saw Cathy and Mark hovering in front of his office. The three looked at each other and sighed. Russell strode forward, boomed out a 'good morning' and opened the door. He didn't look over his shoulder and made straight for the loveseat. He threw himself down and fixed his two business lieutenants.

"Alright, spit it out." Russell said. "What did the junkie do now?"

"Russell, please don't get mad." Cathy tiptoed on her short heels and sat down next to him. "Dynamo has called an emergency board meeting for 12:00pm."

Russell stared at Cathy; his eyes narrowed to wicked slits. "Oh, did he?"

Cathy nodded. "Yes, he said it was important."

"If it's important, I'm sure he told you what it's about." Russell breathed noisily through his nose. "So that we have time to prepare."

Cathy cast a desperate look at Mark who cleared his throat. "Russ, uh, no, Dynamo didn't tell Cathy why."

"Mark, are you going to stand there like a strawman?" Russell watched Mark turn been red as he shuffled over and sat. Russell swallowed and mentally wrapped his arms around his heaving rage. "I'm not going to challenge this decision. I will be in the board room as requested, but that coke-head had better be in the meeting room at 11:59am if we want a civil exchange of words."

Cathy squeezed Russell's hand. "Thanks Russell. I'll make sure to call Dynamo and ask that he be in the building no later than 11:45am."

Russell looked from Cathy to Mark and nodded. He stood up and walked to his desk, sat in his plush chair and turned on the computer. Over the monitor he saw Cathy and Mark trudge silently out of his office and lightly close the door. As the computer booted up Russell leaned back, folded his hands behind his head and stared at the ceiling. He would require the wisdom of all three classes of yogic breathing not to explode. He sat up straight, opened his email and began reading in reverse order of arrival.

The morning was busy with two quick calls with clients, dozens of emails to respond to and a sales report he needed to complete for Cathy. They had big plans to tackle Germany, and next month the two had scheduled client visits to present their company to some important names in the European powerhouse. Rave2Engrave worked almost exclusively in the Americas, and the chance to get a foothold in Europe would provide a significant boost in sales. Many considered Europe a slow, if not dying continent, but Cathy had seen some significant opportunities that a niche company like Rave2Engrave could take advantage of. Just two or three big sales in Germany could bring in an extra twenty percent in revenue.

With a flick of his wrist Russell looked at his watch. It was 11:55am. He stood and swept his gaudy notepad and favourite fountain pen off his desk. He straightened his tie and made for the door. He marched with his best business face on and revelled in each heel click on the tiles. He opened the door with a practiced sweep of his arm and in one motion was in the board room with the door closed behind him. He called out a good morning to the assembled team and he took his place at the head of the table opposite where Dynamo sat, except there was no Dynamo to be seen. Russell made a big show of looking at his watch. It was 11:57am. He sat with his arm crooked for another moment soaking in the stares from Cathy, Mark, John,

Charlotte and even Olivia was in the room. With a flourish, Russell unbuttoned his suit jacket and pushed his shoulders into the chair. He gave the room and blood curdling smile.

"Let me just call Dynamo," Cathy squeaked. She gave her phone a couple of swipes and taps and put it to her ear with a grimace. "Hello, Dynamo? Yes, we're all gathered. Ok, so you'll be onsite in five minutes? Great!" Cathy put down the phone and communicated what had been heard by the entire room. "Dynamo will be here in five minutes."

Russell swept over the participants. The unease was palpable, and he was sure it wasn't just because of his stony silence. Something was troubling the group and this included the bubbly Olivia who fidgeted with her rings and frequently looked at her phone. There were a few fits and starts at conversation, all initiated by Cathy and none that were directed at him. It seemed like an eternity had passed when a smiling Dynamo burst into the room. Russell looked at his watch. It was 12:17am.

"Morning team! So glad you could come on short notice." Dynamo slid into his seat and winked at Olivia. "I won't take up too much of your time, but I have a big announcement. Liv, can you fire up the projector?"

Olivia bounded up and grabbed the controller and the screen came to life. She gave what Russell thought was a forced smile and nodded to Dynamo. "Team, on this page you can see how Dynamo and I have submitted our business plan to NASA in order to be chosen as a strategic partner!"

A crushing silenced flattened the room and everyone in it. The hush was so stricken that it seemed to take even take the wind out of Dynamo's sails. He flicked his eyes across the room and cleared his throat. "Well, team? What do you think? Big news, right?"

"No, Dynamo, this is not big news." Russell's shoulders' rose and fell and he glared across the table. "Your foolish action is an example of recklessness and conveys to the board of directors a complete lack of business sense."

Dynamo blinked and shook his head. "Sorry Russ, I think you're missing the point."

"I don't miss anything, Dynamo." Russell gripped his fountain pen until his knuckles turned white. "I've been in business longer than you've been alive."

"Sure, you have some experience but what we need is new energy." Dynamo's face hardened. "Something an old-timer doesn't have."

And icy tension threatened to choke the room, but Russell had been through worse with Hector Wallace. "When it comes to making a strategic proposal, the great minds of this company meet, discuss, look at the pluses and minuses and decide whether or not to move forward." Russell switched on his poker face. "Let me ask you something, Dynamo. Who did you share your idea with? And where is your plus-minus report? The one your father and I developed to analyse any business venture."

Russell revelled in the impact that naming Peter had on Dynamo. The junkie blanched and licked his lips. "In today's quick business setting writing reports is a waste of precious time."

"Writing reports enables sound strategy and reduces the risk of imprudent actions taken on a whim." Russell turned to Olivia and pointed at the screen. "Olivia, switch that off."

Olivia trembled as she looked from Dynamo to Russell. "I, sure, I mean—."

"Now, Olivia." Russell watched as her trembling manicured finger pressed a button and the screen went dark. He turned to face a purple Dynamo. "Your father's death was a tragic event for all of us in the company. I don't doubt it was worse for you than it was for any of us. But that doesn't excuse the bullshit you are putting us through." Russell let the comment sink in and continued with his power voice the moment he saw Dynamo open his mouth. "Peter and I had forged a relationship over a period of years that saw the employees double and the revenue more than triple. That was done through bold decisions after strategizing with Mark and Cathy. In the last years everything has been double checked with John and Charlotte. Nothing was done without first using each other as a sounding board." Russell leaned forward. "I'm asking you again, Dynamo. Who did you discuss these decisions with before taking them?"

Dynamo swallowed. "I own this company and I can do—"

"Whatever the hell you want with it, right?" Russell slammed his fist on the table and the room flinched. "Is that what you think, Dynamo? That you can undo what you grandfather Walter did and what your father and I did? If that's what you think, then you can sink your ship alone because I'm getting off at the next port with dry feet." Russell stood and buttoned his jacket. "The next port is much closer than you can possibly imagine. Good luck to you, Dynamo."

Russell reached the door with his hand and hid a smile as he heard Dynamo call out. "Russell, who's going to handle the trip to Germany?"

Russell had one foot out of the meeting room and spoke gleefully. "Why, you are, Dynamo. I'm sure you've read the months of industry reports and strategy that Cathy compiled about the German market." As he shut door he spoke through the fissure. "You can take a side trip to visit the European Space Agency in Paris."

Russell whistled as he walked briskly down the hall and stopped for a moment to stand on one leg. His knee felt positively bionic. He strutted to his office, grabbed his briefcase and keys and walked back out closing the door firmly behind him. He trooped down the stairs lightly, smiled and saluted the secretary and pushed through the front door. His swift steps brought him to his car and he had it started before he even closed the door. As he pulled out of the lot he made a Bluetooth call.

"Hi hon, what's up?" Heather's tinny voice greeted him.

“How about lunch?” Russell pushed down on the gas and felt the buzz. “I’m on the way right now.”

“Sounds great.” Russell could feel her impish grin on the sound waves. “What’s the occasion?”

“The start of a new life.”

Heather chucked. “I’m up for that! I’m almost home, but I’ll keep my jacket and shoes on.”

***

Lunch at their favourite Thai restaurant was better than Russell could have hoped for. His green curry was spot on and he even sampled Heather’s Pad Thai which was better than usual. He wondered if it was his mood or if they had changed their cook. After lunch they drove to the harbour front and took a walk in comfortable silence along the pier. Russell walked them to a park bench on a grass rise with a perfect view of the lake.

They sat and Heather put her head on his shoulder. “So, are you ready to jump straight into retirement?”

Russell looked at the gulls hovering over the water. “I’ll go back in a tie up some loose ends to make sure things are as easy as possible for Mark and Cathy.” He shrugged. “As easy as I can make things considering the situation.

“So, you’re not going to Germany?”

“No, Hezzy.” Russell thought he might feel remorse, but he only felt a relief. “I’ll prepare Mark and Cathy and they’ll have to manage the trip with our junior salesman.”

“I’m sure they can do it.” Heather tugged on his jacket. “Honey-bear? Can I ask you something?”

Russell felt her staring up but he kept his eyes unfocused in the distance. “Sure thing, Hezzy.”

“Was there really a Gizmo?”

A seagull flew over head and landed a few feet away from them. The gull seemed to cast them a quizzical sidelong glance and stood motionless for a few moments. The call hopped along a few steps, batted it's wings and took flight. Russell watched the soaring bird effortlessly ride the breeze over the waters. It dipped low before planning over the lake, then caught an updraft and slowly spiraled upwards. The magical dance brought a smile to his face as he hugged Heather whose entire body shook with laughter. It was the first day of the rest of their lives.

*** **End** ***

Also by Enrico Picchi

Steampunk Blues
Steampunk Blues TenebroCity

The Blunt City Chronicles
King Lester The Groovy

The Paramount Sagas
Baroness

The Vigor Crystal Chronicles
The Petulant Robot

Watch for more at enricopicchi.com.

About the Author

Enrico Picchi is an author because one year ago he decided to be one. He sets no limits in writing, and writes fantasy, science fiction, satire, short stories, novellas, mysteries, ghost stories, fables, flash fiction and philosophy. He is the author of The Paramount Sagas short fiction anthology entitled *'Baroness'.*

Read more at enricopicchi.com.

www.ingramcontent.com/pod-product-compliance
Lightning Source LLC
Jackson TN
JSHW082259160525
84508JS00001B/25
* 9 7 9 8 2 3 0 7 9 7 0 8 1 *